DAUGHTER'S FORTUNE

Not A Pirate Book

CHERYL L-G TRENT

Paperback Book ISBN: 979-8-9893170-1-1

Hardback Book ISBN: 979-8-9893170-2-8

Ebook ISBN: 979-8-9893170-0-4

To all the Outsiders leaving a wake in their path.

Summary:

It's got action, adventure, sword fighting, sailing, true love, intrigue, betrayal, murder, and yes, it's a kissing book.

Jeaneau, The Lady Sea Captain, sails tumultuous seas of society. To her port, a mother desperately trying to get her married. To her starboard, the VOC trying to sink her business when she gets hit in the stern with a plot to overthrow a king. Can she survive these battles? And what of the dashing British officer who keeps crossing her bow?

ONE

It's a Man's World

*J*eaneau politely pushed her way through the standing crowd as best as she could in skirts and wedged shoes. She blew the curls around her face out of her eyes and grunted once or twice before reaching her destination. She looked over the wooden banister, beyond the crowded seats below, and then even further to the square where the officials sat. "Couldn't we get a seat?" She sighed to her companion.

"You are not permitted," he replied.

"Well, that is just ridiculous." She harrumphed. "Every day, I find a new place I can't go."

Jean-Pierre smirked. "Wait til they call your name." This was not a statement, this was a moment of anticipated mirth at the look on their faces when they realized who she was.

She smirked back. "That is always an enjoyable moment."

The gentleman to her left looked at her with odd curiosity and she flashed him a brilliant smile that distracted him completely. He began to introduce himself when a great rapping sound silenced the hall.

Far below in the square, a man read silently from a list of charges before clearing his throat and saying, "This session is for charges of smuggling, piracy, and illegal transportation of unauthorized goods."

Jeaneau leaned towards Jean-Pierre. "Are those not all the same thing?"

"They're British," he replied. "Their laws are redundant."

She snorted. "Quite."

The voice below continued, "…including any contestation of fines, levies, and confiscation." The man tipped back his wig to itch his sweating head. "Will Jean…Jean…" He paused, reading the name more closely, and conferring with a colleague. "What is this name?" he quietly asked.

His colleague reviewed the name and said, "I think that is French, but…is that Dutch? Either way, I really don't care for either. Just call it out and get on with it."

The bailiff nodded and continued, "Jean-U Ul-rick-sin"

Jeaneau rolled her eyes but then raised her voice to ring clearly over the crowd. "Aye."

There was an audible shuffling of heads and bodies as they turned their eyes toward the back of the hall. She lifted her fan, waved at the officials, and then gave a small curtsy.

The bailiff looked confused and repeated the name, "Captain John El-rick-son."

She lifted her chin allowing the light to shine on her elegant neck. "It is Captain Jeaneau Elricksen and I am she."

She allowed the usual murmur of astonishment to flow through the crowd but kept a serene smile on her face and looked directly at the presiding judge.

The judge examined her. She was French in features from her high cheekbones and sharp nose but held the height of a Nederman. He waved a hand and then declared, "Please escort the captain to the main floor, so I do not have to bellow."

Exiting through the masses was easier than their original entry. She maintained elegance as she entered the main floor and stood before the presiding official.

He examined her manner of dress and deduced a woman of fine breeding but certainly of the gentry class. Her skin was pale as fresh cream and her hair the color and thickness of a lion's mane with rich, ruddy tones blended with deep golden strands. Nothing about her appearance would suggest she was a sailor let alone the captain of a ship. He glanced at the man standing next to her who was long, lanky, had piercing blue eyes, and was most definitely French. He banged a large rock several times to quiet the hall, then spoke. "You are Captain Jean…You are captain of the Daughter's Fortune?"

"I am," she replied.

"Are you aware of the charges?"

"I am, but they are false."

"You wish to contest the charges?"

"No, they are false."

Blinking hard at her bold yet dulcet tone, he cleared his throat, then requested, "Bailiff please list the charges."

The bailiff cleared his own throat, then said, "The Daughter's Fortune was found in possession of several commodities that were found necessary to his Majesty's Navy and are to be procured. Any refusal is fineable by law."

"But neither I nor my ship are under British rule."

The Bailiff glared at the interruption, but replied, "Firstly, once you set port in British territory you are subject to her laws. Which reminds me, who is your sovereign?"

"The Sea," she said and flashed a smile that got a chuckle from the audience.

"Captain Ulrickshon, only pirates make such claims."

Her smile dropped and her demeanor hardened. "I solemnly swear I am no pirate, but I was born at sea and will likely die at sea."

He rubbed his brow. "Are you Dutch or French?"

"My father is Dutch. My mother—" She stopped speaking when Jean-Pierre squeezed her hand. He silently reminded her that the Brits were almost always at odds with France, and currently in alliance with the Dutch. To mention her French mother or that she was technically catholic would not be the wisest action. The King may be catholic, but the government was still protestant.

"Are you Dutch?"

"Yes. I'm sure my height gave it away. Or was it my hair?"

A mixture of laughter and chuckling rippled through the audience.

The officer glowered at her unamused. "Well then, under current treaties, the Dutch are our allies, and therefore Dutch goods are subject to use by the British for military purposes if necessary."

"And I assume the British Navy is already in need of commandeering commodities."

"In this case...yes."

She worked hard not to let a frown set on her face. "I still wish to do business with the British, but these commodities are spoken for."

"If you do not wish to relinquish your commodities then you can pay the equivalent to the coffers."

"So my profits suffer either way."

"Your profits are of no concern to His Majesty."

"Obviously."

"Madame, I suggest you curb your tongue."

Jeaneau glared at him, but calmly asked, "If I wish to protest these actions?"

"You just did and it is denied. Relinquish the goods or pay the fine. Your ship will remain in port until you do so and will continue to pay the port fee until the issue is resolved." He then motioned to the Bailiff to proceed to the next case.

The Bailiff picked up the next docket, giving her no further acknowledgment.

Jeaneau took in a deep breath, then with both force and grace, exited the chambers.

She waited a good distance from the building before she

started to fume and produce profanities that Jean-Pierre was accustomed to, but not to those she walked past.

"Perhaps curse in French?" he suggested and bowed to passersby who caught snippets of what she said.

They were halfway back to the ship before she had recollected herself and started to make intelligible sense.

"Unbelievable," she said, as she stopped at a cart and purchased a meat pie.

"Not really," Jean-Pierre replied.

"I know." She sighed and took a bite. The pie was noticeably hot, as Jeaneau tried to cool the bite in her mouth. She finished the bite and blew on the rest of the pie. "But it is still despicable."

"Agreed."

She took another bite.

A young street urchin rushed up to her, completely out of breath, and said, "Pardon me, Miss."

Mouth full, she looked down at him quizzically.

"I have a message for you, Ma'am." He brandished an envelope.

She took the letter and opened it. A look of shock crossed over her face, "It's a writ. Our fees have been paid for."

Jean-Pierre stuttered, "By who?"

"It doesn't say."

"How odd and so quickly."

"Well, I will not scoff at fate. If Olav is back with the new hires, we will sail at tide."

Cut of her Jib

*J*eaneau and Jean-Pierre stood at the edge of the ship, watching the new crew members come aboard. She was changed and ready to sail. The sun was blaring, and she could feel it cut through her hat and headscarf.

She tucked the ends of the scarf back into place and glanced at her Bosun, Olav, who stood at her left, arms sternly crossed. "Any issues with the new crew?"

Olav rolled his thick shoulders and replied, "Well they are a poor lot, too young or too old, and all mongrels. At the last minute, I did acquire one strong young man, and his able father for an excellent bargain, but most able bodies have been impressed."

"Does this mean war is coming?"

"It can be," Jean-Pierre answered. "But war can be profitable if you know just what to sell and to whom. Good time to be a savvy merchant."

"Or a pirate," replied Olav. "Pirates do quite well during wartime."

Jean-Pierre peered over with a steely blue stare that chilled Olav's blood and caused his dark skin to turn ashen.

Olav straightened and cleared his throat. "Or more exactly a privateer. A pirate that is legal and all. Just depends on who you are working for." He fearfully looked at his captain, hoping his clarification was sufficient.

Jeaneau's shoulders had tensed, but she showed no other sign of annoyance at the discussion of pirates.

"We did pick up a few women," Olav said, hoping to return to the original conversation. "They seem able enough for most duties. Some even appear well-skilled."

She nodded again and slowly surveyed the whole ship, picking out her new crew members. She saw the women, and the father and son Olav had mentioned. The son was in his twenties, and she could see he had known the sea half his life already by the muscles in his forearms and his tanned skin. The father was a weathered seaman in his forties. She thought of the same lines on her father's face and fussed at her scarves again. She loved the sea, but her mother had drummed into her from an early age to protect her skin.

The young man, Roger, watched the captain move up to the helm, as he worked the ropes with the older man. "We should tell her."

"Who?"

"The captain."

"You will not," Arthur, his superior posing as his father, barked. "We are in disguise for a reason. This is a short trip, and she will never notice."

The cool breeze hit his face and he heard the rustle of loosening sails. He ran his hand along the railing and surveyed the whole ship. The last of the large sails unfurled and he helped lash them into place. The crew also appeared, gathering on the main deck as they finished their duties. They were a diverse crew, both men and women of all races. He saw lanky French, stout Prussians, and minute Italians. It appeared Captain Elricksen had no qualms with hiring from any nation. She claimed to be Dutch, but it was clear her first mate was French.

Perhaps his superior was right. It did not occur to him that, not only did he have to keep their mission covert from any official they may encounter, but from the crew itself. He noted a shift in the crew's demeanor and found his eyes drawn up to the second level where Captain Elricksen stood with her first mate.

"So, it really is a Lady Captain," he heard a crew member say to another. "Never seen a Lady Captain before. Did her husband die and leave her the ship?"

Roger's eyes fell upon the man speaking and noted it was his superior, Arthur, using an accent.

"Nope," replied the other crew member. "It's her ship. Always has been.'

"Blimey, not sure I can take orders from a woman."

"I suggest you do, mate, because there ain't no question. She is the captain."

At this point, the bosun began roll call.

"And a Moor?" he asked.

The crew member nodded, saying, "Black Dutch" and then shouted, "Aye!" when his name was called.

Once roll call was complete, Jeaneau spoke.

"If you are new to this ship, I expect you to follow the rules just as any other sailor. All rations are equal, and no one gets additional shares or favoritism. This includes me. If you have personal items or provisions you have brought on board, please record them with the Quartermaster and he will also store any items of value if you so wish. Any disputes over items will be resolved with the Quartermaster and Bosun. Fraternization is permitted, but if it impedes with your duties or causes issues among the crew, the penalties are harsh, including docks in pay and loss of privileges. Secondly, no one will be forced into congress without full consent of both parties. If this happens and you are found guilty, the punishment is immediate dismissal."

"Dismissal?" asked a sailor. "How do you dismiss someone off a ship at sea?"

Jeaneau glanced coldly out to the water and then back to the sailor. The message was clear and sent an awe of sobering fear through the crew.

She looked back over the crew. "Olav will give you the duty assignments."

Olav moved forward and began calling off duties, as she stepped down the ladder and into the hull below.

Roger carefully moved through the crew and toward her. His advancement was stopped by a hand on his chest. He followed the hand up the arm and to a ruddy face.

Tall in height, they looked very boyish in a loose shirt, waistcoat, and trousers. Their hair was deep red and shaggy, causing it to curl in an unruly manner around his ears. He nervously smiled. "No leaving the deck until duties are called."

"My apologies," Roger replied and stood at the ready.

"Good. Good." He nodded approvingly and took his hand off Roger's chest. Presenting a courteous nod, he introduced himself. "Emmet, Quartermaster."

Roger noted the distinct Scottish accent. "Roger E..." He fought his instinct to give his real name when Olav bellowed, "Roger Smith, Livestock."

Emmet patted him on the chest. "That's you?"

"Yes...Smith..."

"Come along then. I'll show you the way."

Emmet led him to the hold where he found cargo stacked neatly into every available space and a small number of livestock milling in cages and pins.

"Surely not," he muttered.

"Time to work," Emmet declared and handed him a pitchfork. "Hay is for feed and the floor. Make sure you clear the older hay first. Captain hates when the animals get sick from dank quarters."

Emmet left him to work and moved over to a gated section. Pulling out a key, he opened it and began to check inventory. A short time into his work, the captain came in and began to quietly converse with Emmet. Their camaraderie was relaxed and jovial, even as they discussed the status of cargo.

Roger also noticed the Captain had loosened her scarf, revealing a braided mane of reddish blonde hair and pale skin. He went back to his work and didn't turn back until he felt a presence behind him. "You've tended animals before?"

"Yes," he replied and kept shoveling.

"You were good on the ropes, too. How long have you been sailing?"

"Since I was a young man," he answered.

"Interesting, but you were never pressed into the Navy?"

"I..." He was finding it difficult to lie to her. Perhaps because she was a woman. "I hope to captain my own ship someday, like you."

She paused a moment, looking him up and down, then walked over to a large contraption sitting under an intense beam of light. A quick assessment told him it looked like a brewery still of some sort, though he saw no fire to heat the basin. It was massive in size, standing nearly as tall as the room, and fastened to the hull so it did not slide around. He could see that light hit the lower half but could not quite figure out the configuration. She tapped the basin and then drew liquid from the spout into a small cup.

He stopped shoveling and asked, "I thought all rations were shared."

"They are," she answered. "I am checking the quality."

"Isn't it dangerous to brew your own libations on a ship?"

She turned and smiled at him. "Libations?"

"It's a still."

"A distillation system." She spoke.

"Brandy?"

"No, water. It heats water into steam, then collects on the dome. As the steam cools it then becomes water again over here." She offered the cup. He took the cup and sipped. It was warm and mildly salty, but drinkable water.

"So you made water into water?"

"Saltwater into drinkable water."

He raised a brow. "Saltwater."

She reached over and wrenched open a lid revealing a second container inside, then she pulled back a lid on this container and ran her finger along the rim. When she removed her hand, she displayed fingers covered in a white crust. "Salt for the cook and water for the crew."

"A strange practice for a captain."

"Crews need water."

"Most captains purchase it."

"Why purchase what is all around you?"

He walked over and studied the contraption, "How did you..."

"When I was once in a rainforest, I watched a boy drink water that had collected in a giant leaf. One very hot and boring afternoon I watched water rise in a bottle and then rain back down. On another cool morning, I ran my finger along the bottom of a sail and noticed the water was not as salty. If you look long enough, you notice how nature works and eventually you can figure out how to mimic it."

He remained silent contemplating her statement, but his fascination for this peculiar woman grew. The ship and its captain were unconventional but appeared to work. He knew being on a merchant ship would be different from his knowledge of military life, but this world seemed alien. He went back to the stall and began shoveling. "And your rules."

"Yes?"

"You allow…fraternization."

"Yes."

"Does it not cause discourse?"

"I've found not allowing it causes greater discourse."

Emmet stepped over. "Captain, the cook has his cut for tonight's rations. I'm assuming you are taking the night watch?"

"Yes, if I get a chance to rest," Jeaneau replied, unwinding her scarf and pulling off her gloves, exposing the top of her fitted jacket that was cut in a man's style but fitted to her curves.

"You do that. The Limey and I have this under control."

He watched the captain leave then looked at Emmet. "I'm not from Lime."

Emmet laughed. "Fair 'nuff. Then I'll just call ya Young Smith."

Roger looked at him quizzically.

"Well, you came with your father, didn't you? He can be Old Smith and you can be Young Smith."

"I would not consider myself old," Arthur gruffed as he climbed down the ladder. "Plenty of years left in these bones."

"Well, you can be Smith then, but he's still Young Smith."

"Agreed," replied Arthur. "You are the Quartermaster?"

"I am," he replied.

"I have a package I'd like kept secure."

"Fine." Emmet grabbed the manifest.

Arthur handed over a large sack.

"Clothes?" Emmet asked.

"For the misses," he said with a wink, "rather not have them thrown about before they get to her."

"Okay then." Emmet peered at the package. "I'll need to examine them."

"I'd rather you not. They are…" Arthur leaned in, "unmentionables."

"Ooooh," replied Emmet, giving an understanding nod. "All the same, I should look."

Arthur put his hand firmly on the package. "Her son is right there. I promise. It's just some lady things I promised to get her. Don't need these men rummaging around in them and getting dirty and stains on them."

Emmet waivered. "I suppose not." He took the package, tagged it, and secured it on a shelf.

Arthur returned a friendly grin, "Appreciated." and went back to his work.

Arthur snickered as he passed Roger. "Enjoy the muck, Son."

THREE

Winds of the North Sea

Roger knew the duty was meant to instill humility, but cleaning a stall was nothing new to him. Once his work was done, Emmet told him where the crew ate and left him to clean before repast.

He changed his shirt, put on the civilian coat he boarded in, and cleaned himself as etiquette required. When he finally made his way to the dining area, he found everyone already seated and in all manner of undress. Olav and Emmet sat with unbuttoned waistcoats and Jean-Pierre had no waistcoat at all. They lounged in their chairs and enjoyed their meal. Other members of the crew lighted where they could.

"Young Smith," Emmet declared. "Don't you look posh. Come sit at the table."

Roger did not let his remarks embarrass him and simply sat down to eat. He noted the captain was not present. When he noticed movement at the door he assumed it was her, but another man stepped in. He was small and meek in comparison with the rest of the crew, including Emmet. His hair was short and mousey grey in color. However, unlike the rest of the officers, he was fully dressed and very clean in appearance.

"Lance!" Jean-Pierre declared. "You have showered us with your presence. Have you met the Young Smith?"

Roger stood out of respect and bowed to Lance.

Lance offered a deep nod in return. "Young Smith, is it not?"

"For the moment," replied Roger.

"I am Lance Helmsmith. The resident surgeon."

"I wasn't aware this ship had one."

"The captain believes in maintaining the health of all on board, so she has me. On that subject, I will need to see you at your convenience to ensure there are no…issues."

Jean-Pierre snorted at this and grinned as he took a long sip from his mug.

The doctor timidly continued, "We can't have things spread among the crew that can slow us down."

"I assure you I will not be spreading anything whilst aboard the ship."

"Lance," Olav jibed, "you should probably check Jean-Pierre, again. I believe he was at the brothel house."

Jean-Pierre gawked at his friend. "We were at the Courthouse."

Olav laughed. "Still a dirty place where deals are made behind doors and money changes hands!"

The room burst into laughter.

"Oh!" Lance proclaimed, his voice raising in pitch. "Not what I meant, good sir, but the simplest ailment can wreak havoc in small quarters if not contained. You and your father should have seen me immediately. Heaven only knows what miasma possibly came aboard when you arrived."

"I will see you when you are next available, but I assure you that my health is strong and unhindered."

He nodded and sat down to eat. "Then there should be no worries."

Roger sat again and proceeded to eat and listen to the conversation. There were times that they asked him questions, but he mainly let them discuss among themselves and observed their manners. He found Olav and Jean-Pierre to be the rather gregarious members of the group while Lance remained more reserved in conversation. Emmet's demeanor was the most chaotic. He would jump and start at the slightest thing to then settle down into quiet disconnected moments. He concluded, while they all appeared to be typical sailors, there was something distinctly different about them that was hidden underneath. He decided that this mystery would reveal itself with time.

They slipped out of English waters and into the North Sea. Heading up to his next duty, Roger found the captain staring intently at the hills. He followed her gaze but was unsure what she was looking at.

"The wind," she said softly. "Watch how it moves."

He looked back at the hills and saw the wind start at the top. As it moved, it pressed all the grass down flat, and instead of whipping straight down the slope, it wound itself back and forth like a snake. He could almost hear it slither. Its force did not stop as it hit the water but continued to wind across the surface until it slammed into the hull with great force. He jolted in surprise from the hit.

She turned and gave him a small grin. "How often do you sail the North Sea?"

"More often than desired," he replied.

"Any other waters?"

"Many."

"Have you ever known any other water like her?"

"I have not."

She nodded in agreement. "Neither have I. It's as if the wind is living in these waters and has its way with the land and sea. But she must be crossed to enter the Nederlands. Makes you wonder how the Vikings ever decided to journey past her."

"From what I understand, very little stopped the Vikings."

"Indeed. My father says a sailor's will must be stronger than the wind of the North Sea or she will break it."

"When was the first time you sailed her?"

She grabbed the ends of her scarf that the wind had torn loose and replied, "I was born on this sea."

Jean-Pierre called her name. She gave Roger a friendly smile and walked away.

FOUR

Choppy Waters

___

Jean-Pierre sipped softly from his cup and glanced at Jeaneau, who quietly chewed her dinner. "Are you going to come to the officer's table at all?"

She looked up at him. "Do I need to?"

"Well, your company is appreciated."

She shrugged softly. "The table is a bit crowded. I was being considerate."

"You're avoiding him," he retorted.

She peered at him. "I most certainly am not."

"I've watched you. If he comes near, you make polite conversation and then find a reason to be elsewhere. Does he unsettle you?"

"Yes, every time I see him it's like he wants to say something but doesn't."

"Oh?"

She nodded and kept eating. "I was also thinking," she said, changing the subject, "it was too easy for the port authority to attempt to seize our cargo, and then some mysterious stranger paid our fees. I keep wondering how convenient it was."

"You were the one that said not to scoff at fate."

"And why are the British confiscating provisions? Didn't they just put a Catholic King on the throne? That should make them ally with France."

"A Catholic King who is building an Army. Perhaps another war with the Dutch?"

"But aren't Charles and William related?"

"And family doesn't bicker?"

She snorted. "True, but I would think Louis' ambition would be more of a concern."

"No matter the course, it could be lucrative. Conflict is always profitable."

"But at what cost? How many of our crew? My father's crew have suffered from being impressed. I don't wish to fight for the Dutch, the French, or anyone else. I just want to sell our wares."

"And when the countries finally go to war and the only people buying our wares are the military?"

A scornful frown drew across her face.

Jean-Pierre smirked. "Ah, you know I am right." He leaned forward. "Jeaneau, war is inevitable. Fighting it will only cause us more grief. I say, if opportunity presents itself, let us profit from it. You know the VOC will."

His last comment made her sit up straight, but he was right. The United East India Trading Company would not hesitate to use war to gain a stronger hold over trade. Their trading house struggled as it was. For the VOC to gain more power over the water would mean more pressure to join the coalition or to fold. She dropped her fork and knife and crossed her arms.

Jean-Pierre let her fume for a moment as her own stubborn will battled with the logic of the argument. He gently sipped and watched her face contort as she contemplated every avenue until logic won out. He knew he could speak again when she picked up her dinnerware and continued to eat, though now there was a level of anger in every jab at the plate of food. "So let's make allies, not enemies."

$\mathcal{R}$oger woke after first sleep, noticing a change in the ship's movements. He put on his coat and moved to the upper deck. Standing on the main deck, bathed in moonlight, was the captain. Her eyes were locked on a spot far out to sea. She wasn't wearing her scarves, and her hair was loose, writhing in the wind. He walked up the steps, and without speaking, gazed in the same direction.

In the distance, he saw flashes of light highlighting dark clouds and an ominous sheet of black falling from the sky. He took in a deep breath and smelled the wind, then checked its direction. "We should not encounter it."

She nodded. "Unless the winds change."

They both stood silently observing the storm, watching the flashes of light flicker and thrill their senses. Each found peace as they gazed out to sea and did not want to interrupt its performance. Eventually, they both felt a familiar ease develop between them and began to relax. Roger leaned against the railing and accepted the offered drink when Jeaneau pulled it from a slit in her skirts.

He finally asked, "So you were born here?"

She sipped and nodded. "And during a storm. My father said that when my mother went into labor, a storm brewed around us and grew with her pain. When she finally brought my brother into the world, lightning hit the deck and cracked a dinghy in two. When I came into the world, the storm suddenly stopped and the moonlight broke into the cabin to say hello."

"You have a twin brother?"

She nodded and tried to hide her grimace.

"Is he alive?"

"Last time I saw him," she said with a bitter tone.

He shifted and examined her face. "I will not ask further."

She looked down at her decanter. "Thank you."

They continued to watch the storm until the ship drifted past and then, without speaking, went their separate ways.

On the last leg of the voyage, Jeaneau invited all the sailors to the Captain's Quarters for dinner. The dinner was jovial and Jean-Pierre watched Jeaneau display an ease around the new sailor that she didn't afford many.

The meal stretched long into the night. One by one, the sailors excused themselves until Roger noticed it was just him, Emmet, who had fallen asleep in his chair, and Jeaneau.

Jeaneau had her back to him and was looking through her collection of books for one pertaining to their conversation. His breath hitched, watching her skirts shift around her hips as she twisted and contorted to reach for the book. He abruptly stood, knocking his chair to the floor. "Captain," he replied curtly, "it has been an honor to dine with you, but I must retire."

Bewilderment crinkled her brow and pursed her mouth. "Very well then," she replied and handed him the book. "Then you are welcome to read this at your leisure. Until we dock."

He took the book and bowed politely. "Captain Elricksen."

Her throat was tight, but she politely replied, "Mr. Smith."

FIVE

Sea of Obligations

eaneau was deeply engrossed in supervising the unloading of the ship when she felt someone standing behind her. She turned, expecting Jean-Pierre, but was surprised to find her father. "Papa!"

He embraced her in a strong hug and then kissed her cheek.

"What are you doing here? I would have met you at the storehouse."

"You were delayed, so I wanted to make sure there was nothing wrong. The ship looks unharmed."

She sighed and brushed back her scarf. "Our delay was not technical. It was political."

"Political?"

"Yes…" she looked about before deciding whether to divulge but thought otherwise upon seeing Roger and his father step on deck. "Mr. Smith."

Roger politely bowed to Jeaneau and the man standing next to her. He was a massive man in the later years of life and had the same wild mane as Jeaneau.

"Mr. Smith, this is Elrick, my father, and owner of our shipping company."

23

"It is a pleasure to meet you, sir. You have a fine ship and a fine captain."

"Why, thank you. Are you new to the crew?"

"Only for this trip. My father and I have business here in Amsterdam."

Jeaneau, unaware of this information, frowned slightly.

Elrick said, "Too bad. It becomes harder and harder to find able sailors these days."

"It is a fine ship, and if needed, we will look for her again." He looked from Elrick to Jeaneau and produced the book she had lent him. "Captain Elricksen, thank you for your assistance and I wish you the safest passage in any future travels."

She grasped the book and gave a solemn grin. "Thank you, Mr. Smith."

Roger and Arthur bowed again and walked off the ship.

Elrick looked at his daughter. "So what was the delay?"

She gestured to Jean-Pierre to take over duties. "I will explain later."

Elrick put an arm around his daughter's shoulders, holding her close as they walked off the ship. "Was he the delay?"

She gave him a look.

He chuckled. "He was very English."

"Very," she replied. "How is Mother?"

"In France." He felt relief wash over his daughter and chuckled. "She did leave a letter for you."

The tension returned. "Investors?"

"Investors."

*R*oger and Arthur walked off the ship and headed toward a billeting house. Once in the room, Arthur opened the satchel that had been stored under lock and key on the ship and pulled out its contents. They were not lady's clothes, but two fine suits. He handed Roger his suit and unfurled his own attire. Arthur checked the contents tucked away in his pocket, verifying the letter was still bound and sealed.

Slipping it back inside, he declared, "Now that we are here, I need an audience with Billy."

"How do we do that?" Roger asked.

"We have an introduction. Once we are introduced, we will produce the letter. I've been told this is mere formality. Billy is ready to aid."

"And your role in all of this?"

"We hope my history is sufficient enough to garner favor?"

"And if that doesn't work?"

Arthur chuckled. "We beg?"

*J*eaneau worked her way through the crowded party in her usual fashion. This morning she was captain of a ship, tonight she was a lady of influence. A smile played on her painted lips and her cheeks shone red from the heat of the room. She rarely got far before she was stopped by gentlemen, young and old, most inquiring about the mundane and polite. Anything to garner her attention.

She spoke to everyone with charm and grace and always seemed to be able to move from one to the other without losing tact. When she was at the prow of her ship, her sole goal was to get from one port to the next safe and sound. When she donned powder and flourished a fan, her sole goal was to ensure every man in the room desired her so greatly, they would agree to anything.

"Mademoiselle Jeaneau, when will you stop risking your life and stay safely in port?" one would say.

"Oh, I know not," she would reply with a gentle sigh. "Surely, when I know the future of our company no longer needs me to sail?"

"What would that entail?"

"I certainly cannot leave when we have so few ships. We need funds for more ships and more captains to sail them."

"And if such funds are acquired?"

"Then I could perhaps settle." This was a lie, but they need not know it.

"Mlle. Jeaneau, what will it take to tame such a lady as you?" another would say.

"Does such a man exist that can shower me with the same love and riches as the sun and sea?" she would reply.

"Mlle. Jeaneau, perhaps I should be like King Alf and come after the beautiful Alvilda."

"Am I worthy of such a hunt? I am neither a pirate nor a princess."

She continued in this manner long into the night, each time leaving them with hope. Which, in turn, would lead them to find her father and discuss the future of the business and her.

Her father greeted each man with jovial interest and made arrangements for investments into the business, while providing words of encouragement, saying he would speak of them in high favor with his daughter.

Social gatherings could be both small and quaint or grand and crowded. Tonight was the latter. Such assemblage made it easy to avoid those you did not wish to converse with while staying quite distracted by those you did. Parties of this size also meant a tremendous rise in indoor temperatures and a sense of claustrophobia that made tight ship quarters seem pleasant smelling and spacious.

As the night carried on, Jeaneau found a moment to escape outside for a breath of fresh air. While she did not personally enjoy the fashionably low-cut bodice of evening wear, she did enjoy feeling the cool breeze on her chest. Sweat dripped and pooled down her cleavage causing her to shiver. She closed her eyes and inhaled deeply, leaning against the cold stone.

Her solitude was disrupted by fingers trailing up her arm. She flinched and whirled on the person, so bold to touch her without request, and found a very familiar face smirking back at her.

"Rafe!" she proclaimed and hit him with her fan.

He laughed and without permission wrapped his arms around her waist. "Mlle. Jeaneau, when will you let me make an honest woman of you?"

She playfully pushed away his reach for a kiss and replied, "That would require you to become an honest man."

He scoffed and wriggled his eyebrows. "Then let's leave this place and do dishonest things."

She laughed and did not fight him when he began kissing her neck. He pushed her back against the wall and drew closer. Part of her enjoyed him, while the other half ensured that they remain in solace and not seen.

His hand dove into the hidden slits of her skirts, that he knew existed, and ran across her thigh, up to her rump. Exhausted from a night of socializing it was easy to let Rafe invoke pleasure. As his hand began to inch up her petticoats, she found it difficult to resist, but gently pushed him away.

In a breathy tone, she asked, "What are you doing here?"

He leaned back in and nibbled her ear. "Just as you. Politics."

Giggling, she slipped under his arms, and back into the light. "I do not politick."

"Do not play innocent with me, Mademoiselle. I know your ambitions and charms."

She flicked her fan at him, scoffing at his accusations.

He grabbed her wrist and pulled her back into the darkness. "Do not deny it. How many of these men know you will never marry?"

She grinned and toyed with the ruffle around his neck. "I never said I wouldn't marry."

His finger tapped her lip in judgement. "But you will never be put to port."

Shrugging, "True, the sea is my life. Why should I stay on land if I marry?"

"Because it's what a respectable woman would do."

She laughed. "Well, I'm certainly not that."

"No," he said, drawing in her lips for a kiss, "you are not."

After a long moment, she reluctantly broke their embrace. "It seems we both have work to do."

He groaned softly and let her go. "Will I see you after?"

"Perhaps…" she said with a sly grin, brushing her fan across his cheek before slipping back inside.

Rafe leaned against the wall and waited before returning. Jeaneau had an effect on him and the rest of the party did not need to see it. When he stepped back into the busy hall, he found his charges, two English officers conversing with members of the Hague. While the older gentlemen seemed comfortable conversing, the second, Roger, remained quiet and observant.

He saw the young man's eyes move away from the stodgy

old men and across the room. Rafe followed his gaze and smirked. The young man was staring directly at Jeaneau.

Jeaneau was lost in her art of persuasion, shining brightly and capturing the attention of those around her. Oddly, Roger's face did not carry the expected look of adoration, instead, he frowned.

Rafe approached the young man and glanced over at Jeaneau. "Is the lady not to your liking?"

Roger looked at Rafe. "Pardon?"

"The young woman over there."

"Do you know her?" Roger inquired.

"I do. She is well known here in certain circles."

"Certain circles?" Roger asked.

"Actually…several circles, but mainly as the eligible daughter of a shipping magnate. If you can tame her."

"Tame her?"

Rafe hemmed and hawed as he searched for the best word. "She's a bit of a coquette. There are a few men here hoping for her favor, but…"

"It would be beyond most to satisfy her?"

"Yes," Rafe said with a small surprise. "Do you know women like her?"

Roger rolled his glass in his hand. "No, I am certain I know no one like her."

Arthur clapped his hand on Roger's shoulder and asked, "Distracted, my friend?"

Rafe chuckled. "She is that."

"Isn't that the Lady Captain?" Arthur inquired.

"Oh? You do know Captain Elricksen?"

"We have had the opportunity," Roger politely replied.

"Oh well." Rafe scratched his nose. "She has many admirers. She also has the eyes of your associates on her."

"How so?" Roger asked.

"Her father's shipping company. They are not part of the VOC."

"But they are Dutch," Roger replied.

"And independent. Likely due to her mother's French ties."

Arthur scratched his chin. "I have a feeling few men tell her what to do."

Rafe sighed. "But we are still compelled to try…"

SIX

Tricky Navigation

As the sun began to gray the sky that morning, Jeaneau took in a deep breath and rose from the bed. Skillfully untangling her limbs from Rafe's, she pulled her chemise back over her shoulders. As she sat up and ran her fingers through her hair, she felt a hand on her arm.

"Leaving so soon?"

"I do have a reputation to uphold."

"Nonsense." He drew her back into the bed and ran his hands across her waist and over her hips. "If I am correct, all anyone knows is you returned to your ship last night, and if anyone asks, every man on that ship will attest to it."

She smirked. "They would."

"You are a good captain."

Her head quirked at his remark. "Oh?"

"It is well known among the right circles that you run a fine ship. Woman or not."

She sighed, "Why is being a woman a factor in how I lead?"

He kissed her shoulder. "Simply is."

She stared at him carefully. "What circles have you been in

to discuss me? Have you been talking to my father? Or worse, my mother?"

"Good Lord, no. Your father would be happy if you never saw me, and your mother would not consider me a fine enough marriage."

"True…so who have you been speaking with?"

He pulled his arms away, tucking them behind his head. "I told you I was there last night because of politics."

"Yes."

"Are you aware that William is building up his Dutch reserves?"

"So?"

"He plans to move those reserves very soon, and to do so, he needs ships."

"And?"

"The VOC is willing to provide those ships."

Jeaneau's eyes widened, and her face flushed, "But they could use more ships and they want mine." She sat up violently. "They want us to join the VOC!"

He sat up and reached for her. "Jeaneau…"

"No, I see." She stood and began to rummage for her smalls. "You influence me, so I will influence my father. We do not want to join the VOC. We like being independent."

"Times are changing, Jeaneau. The VOC and others like it are controlling the seas. If you don't join, they will destroy you."

"Join the VOC and do their bidding?" She clutched her chest passionately. "It is our company and my ship. We choose what we ship and how we conduct our business."

"You would still have those freedoms."

She scoffed and put on her slippers. "You have already said they need more ships to carry troops. Who do they plan to attack? And when they do, will that side care that my crew are not soldiers?" She whipped her dress off the floor and put it on. "Let's not even discuss the percentage the VOC will expect for joining their little league." She began to grumble and curse under her breath as she scrounged for her pair of bodies.

Exasperated, he beseeched. "Simply talk to them."

"No," she said, brandishing her found pair of bodies at him. Her hair crowned her face in wild tangles. "You tell them what we have told them before. Elricksen Shipping is an independent shipping company that does not need the VOC, or any other force, to keep them afloat. Elricksen's have sailed the waters since the age of our ancestors, and we will sail until our bloodline is no more."

Roger and Arthur stood outside a small drawing room waiting to meet with their intended purpose.

"William is a fighting man like you and me," Arthur began. "He's been fighting and running an army from an early age. He is the reason the Netherlands are not part of France or England. When other Dutch officials fled, he stood his ground. He has a great dislike for the French and catholic motives."

"And Catholics?"

"No...I wouldn't say directly for Catholics, just their politics. He's a Calvinist."

"His true distaste is Louie and he doesn't want to see England ally with France."

The doors to the side opened and they were escorted into a smaller room where a man sat behind a dark wood table covered in papers. His hair was set in the stylish manner of nobles, dark long ringlets, split in the center with high peaks. His nose was sharp and large, affording him a sternness that counteracted his large eyes and arched brows. His eyes also carried the weariness of a man serving his country. He was William, Prince of Orange, and Stadtholder. Roger was standing in front of the ruler of the Netherlands and the person in direct line to be the ruler of England.

William looked up and addressed Arthur. "Former Rear Admiral Arthur Herbert of the English Navy, what brings you to these foreign lands?"

"I am here to deliver a message."

"My advisors tell me that it is a very important message. Is it by voice or written?"

"It is written." Herbert produced the letter and handed it over.

William took the letter. "Have you read this?"

"I have."

"Have you, sailor?"

"Lt. Roger Edevane, Your Excellency. No, I have not."

"This is a letter of treason. It wants me to assist parliament in overthrowing the King of England."

All color drained from Edevane's face, but he remained silent. Ignorance was no longer a refuge.

William looked at Arthur. "So seven members of the English Parliament have penned their grievance into immortality, and they trust you to deliver their message." He examined Arthur intently. "My Uncle stripped you of all your positions, did he not?"

Arthur stiffened but was prepared for this. "He has."

"You were a high-ranking member of parliament, higher than some of the men who signed this letter."

"I was."

"Some say you lost over 4,000 annum for simply not agreeing to the King's wishes."

"What he asked went against my morals. I could not serve under good conscience."

"A man of conscience and conviction?" He rolled up the

letter. "I assume there is good reason that you have delivered this letter, and not a mere errant messenger."

"Yes, I wish to offer my services."

"Your services?"

"Yes, let me lead your naval fleet. You are a great commander on land, but I know the sea. If you plan to finally stand up against your uncle, let me sail your ships. I know the best ports for landing, and I still have the support of the navy sailor."

William looked at Roger. "I assume you are proof of his naval support."

Roger Edevane stood erect, working to show no emotion. "I believe that is my purpose."

William folded his hands on the desk. "Lord Herbert, I am sure you will lead my Navy with assuredness, but you are brash and ruffle feathers. Conviction or not, how can I be certain that you will not refuse my commands?"

"By oath, of course. You serve the people, and I will serve you."

William picked the letter back up and handed it to Herbert, "I will be in The Hague tomorrow. Present this letter to me then, Lord Admiral."

"Yes, my liege."

SEVEN

Breakwater

*J*eaneau bounded onto her ship and straight into her quarters. When Jean-Pierre peered through the cracked door, he could see she was fuming. Clothes flew left and right. Lids slammed and containers clanked. He pushed open the door and leaned against the frame. "How was your evening?"

"My evening?" She tossed petticoats into a chest, but the voluminous layers stuck halfway out. "My evening was fine; it was my morning that could have gone better."

He fought a rising smirk. "The morning light shone a little too harshly?"

She snorted, pulling him in and slamming the door shut. "So beguiling." Stripping off her fine chemise, she put on her day clothes, starting with her shift and woolen stockings. She fiddled with the garter ties around her waist. "Lure me to bed then try to take my ship."

"Take the ship?" Jean-Pierre asked while handing her a pair of bodies. "Who wants to take the ship, now?"

She slipped them on and glowered. "The VOC."

He chuckled and started tightening the laces. "The VOC lured you to bed to take your ship?"

She let out a defeated sigh. "Rafe."

Jean-Pierre clucked his tongue.

She groaned softly. "I know. He always has an agenda…"

"So, he is working for the VOC?"

"Apparently," she grumbled.

"What do they want with us?"

She lunged over and grabbed her petticoats. "It seems the Orange Prince plans to be King."

"And?" he asked, fighting her laces as she put on skirts.

"And he needs ships to carry his precious army across the sea."

It was Jean-Pierre's turn to sigh. "And the VOC sees this as an opportunity to absorb new ships into their ports."

"Precisely." She fastened her skirts and grabbed her jacket. "I'm sure they wish to lure us in with offers of bounties, port access, and permanent shipping assignments."

"Which all sound dreadful…" Jean-Pierre mocked.

"You taunt, but that also means cuts and fees taken from our pockets to line theirs. Stricter regulations on cargo and crew, and don't forget the assigned militia!"

"Well, that we could do without."

She pulled out her scarves and began to wrap them around her head. "And they tried this time on the tip of a cock. I'm a fool."

Jean-Pierre suppressed his laughter. "At least more pleasurable than their other attempts."

She rolled her eyes at him and began to clean up her quarters. What was previously tossed was now being carefully flattened and folded. Her anger faded, and somber thoughts took its place.

Jean-Pierre picked up a stray pair of drawers and assisted. "He's just a man. I'm sure he was more interested in wetting his wick than his assignment."

"Rafe knows better," she grumbled.

Jean-Pierre nodded in agreement and carefully folded her dress. "But he has to work, and his work is persuasion."

"Persuasion of others," she snapped as she started matching and rolling stockings. "Not me. He knows he cannot fool me in that manner."

Jean-Pierre set the dress to the side of the chest and began to pull the other jumbled items from the trunk. "But it is in his nature to try. The mere fact that you are not persuaded so easily makes you all the more...you are a more enticing challenge."

"Oh, so you think he wishes to best me?"

"You are both a challenge and a reward. If he bests you, then his reward is you."

She snorted in disbelief. "I do not wish to be some man's prize, Jean-Pierre. I am not some fat goose available to the highest bidder."

He paused and looked at her. "But you play with these men and make them think just that."

"Because it is good for business. Men put money into the company hoping for a particular return on their investment."

"Eventually, someone will want that return."

She folded a smock and ran her hand slowly over the embroidered edge. "I have time til then." But her lie was evident to them both.

"Jeaneau, eventually you will be forced to choose."

"Why? How is it that a man can live his life as he pleases, but a woman cannot?"

"Don't fool yourself. A man has just as many obligations as a woman."

"But his choices are greater and farther reaching."

"For most," Jean-Pierre agreed, "but not all. And you do have rights and freedoms."

"I do right now, but eventually, I will be forced to marry, and then what?"

"Jeaneau, do you truly believe your father would ever force such a contract upon you?"

Glowering, she admitted the truth. "No…but mother might."

He chuckled. "And if she tries, you can take to the seas like Avilida and ne'er be seen again."

She let out a laugh and leaned into her friend. He stroked her hair and kissed the top of her head.

"You could just marry me," she said, "and we will never have to worry again."

He chortled. "Wouldn't that be a marriage. I believe the two of us would have trouble finding satisfaction between the sheets."

"When has sex ever been a factor in marriage?"

"True," he said, holding her in a warm embrace, "but it's an excellent benefit."

*L*t. Edevane followed his commander out of the estate and back into the carriage. He waited for it to begin moving before speaking. "Sir, I have the greatest respect for you, and when you were my commander I followed you into battle without question."

"I'm aware, Lt. But?"

"But this is more than asking for aid. This is tantamount to mutiny."

"It's only mutiny if we fail."

"It is still mutiny."

Herbert shifted in his seat and scratched under his wig. "When the times call for it, sometimes mutiny is the only course of action."

"Sir, I understand your pride…"

"My pride has nothing to do with it!" Arthur bellowed. He paused for a moment and took a breath. "King James threatens everything parliament has tried to establish for England's people, and now he has a son. He is a papist and wishes to push his ideals on a land that does not wish to be under the thumb of the catholic church. Billy is more of an intellectual and will bring England further into the light, and not back into the dark ages."

"I understand your motives, but why was I not informed? I was told to assist my former commander in sailing to the Netherlands. I was not told I'd be assisting in the overthrow of my sovereign."

"You were told, because I requested you."

Edevane straightened. "Sir?"

"I chose you, Lt. You are smart and are able to make a quick decision, but you also follow orders. It is why you did not falter in your loyalty, even now when you learned of my actions. It is an admirable quality and will do you well as captain."

"Captain?"

Herbert nodded. "You are to sail back with me to England in command of one of the ships carrying our soldiers. Once we succeed, you will be given your own ship. I believe I commanded my first ship at your age."

"And if it fails…"

"Then I say you were merely following the orders you were given. Any action in the plot was unbeknownst to you."

"Until this moment it was, but now…I do not know if my conscience will allow it."

"Roger, there are times when you must steer directly into the tempest in order to cut through it. Fighting on the side of William may be a gamble, but the payoff is a better life for you and England."

EIGHT

Fata Morgana

*J*eaneau climbed up to the crow's nest and looked to where the sailor pointed. In the distance, was a ship approaching fast and flying Portuguese colors. "How many guns?"

"At least one tier."

"What is the crew doing?"

"Prepping cannons. The sails are full, but they are setting up the rigging for a hard turn."

She frowned. "She's faster."

"We could be lucky, and she is merely taking precautions."

"Then we do the same." Peering down to the quarterdeck, she motioned to Olav to prepare the guns.

He read her signal and bellowed orders. Gauging the direction of the other ship, she sent Jean-Pierre the signal to change their course and worked her way back down, as sailors shimmied up to loosen sails.

Her feet hit the ground with a thud, and she ran up to the quarterdeck. "Lift the covers!" she barked. Her order was passed along, and she could hear the shutters of the cannon ports open.

"Too fast?" asked Jean-Pierre, handing over the wheel.

"And readying her guns," she replied.

"Hopefully, opening the shutters will fool them."

Jeaneau nodded in hope because they both knew there were no cannons and simply black squares of paint under those shutters.

"Pirates?"

"Portuguese Flag. Likely privateers."

"Ship?"

"Sloop and riding high. They will catch us."

He frowned. "So why did we bank starboard?"

She pointed at the sky. "See the plume?"

"Are you mad?" He gaped.

"They are riding too high. We will fare the storm better."

"We could still be caught or lose a mast."

"Better than losing the whole ship. I will not simply sit here like a duck and be plucked."

"Aye, Aye, Captain."

As the Daughter's Fortune drove into the growing storm, the Portuguese ship drew closer. The crew split their work between sails and priming the small batch of guns.

Jeaneau entered her cabin and secured her logs.

Emmet entered and breathlessly asked, "Orders?"

"Pull any remaining weapons from the cage and load it with vital cargo. Have Lance prep his table."

He nodded and rushed down below. Jeaneau closed books and locked cabinets, then began to change her clothes. She threw off her jacket and pulled on a front-lacing pair of bodies that was stiff and molded to fit close to her frame. She then put back on her coat and buttoned it two-thirds of the way up. Jean-Pierre popped his head in.

She turned, glancing at him, as she tucked her scarves under the collar of her coat. "Is it the ship?"

His eyes were wide and filled with bewilderment. "You have to come see this."

She bounded toward the topside and looked for the ship

behind them. It was gaining ground, but not on them yet. She turned to gauge the storm. It was developing as expected but had a strange dark horizon that she was lost in understanding. "What is that?"

Jean-Pierre gazed in bafflement. "I don't know."

Olav scratched his chin. "Storm wall?"

Jeaneau shook her head. "It doesn't look right?"

"Well," Jean-Pierre shrugged. "We can either sail into it and find out, or deal with the Tugas."

Jeaneau peered into the storm and considered her best course. She had to decide if the strange storm was more or less dangerous than being boarded and raided of all their cargo. Her crew could stand and likely fight off the brigands, and they were able to sail through the harshest of storms, but which would bring a greater loss of life? In the end, it was her gut that made the decision. Despite her willingness to stand and fight, something told her to head for the storm.

"Remain on course."

"Aye," the crew replied in unison, without hesitation.

They were on the edge of the storm now and could only see the rain falling, obscuring the original dark horizon they had seen earlier. The wind snapped against the sails, keeping the crew busy.

Olav had the guns prepped but covered to keep the powder from getting wet.

Daughter's Fortune broke into the curtain of rain and found the storm to be navigable.

Jeaneau watched the other ship which was now nearly upon them. "We need bigger swells!"

"I can't make the storm more dangerous," Jean-Pierre retorted.

"Then what good are you?" she quipped back. She turned and put her hand on Jean-Pierre who was at the wheel and holding the ship steady. "You know the ship. Follow the storm and ride her hard. Hopefully, their helmsman is not as able as you."

He smiled. "Aye, Captain."

Jeaneau moved down the quarterdeck and across the ship encouraging the crew in their tasks and shoring up any lines. The storm now howled in their ears and made it difficult to converse. She felt the weight of the rain weigh down on her hat and tore it off. The wind whipped at her scarves, but they kept most of the rain from her face.

She was helping tack a sail for speed when she felt a hand on her shoulder. It was a sailor and he pointed toward the helm. There she saw Jean-Pierre and Olav shouting at her. She rushed back to the quarterdeck and looked for the ship. As she suspected, it was struggling with the storm and had to tack most of its sails, causing it to fall back.

Olav came to her side and bellowed, "That's not the problem!"

She gave him a baffled glance and then followed his pointing finger. She turned around fully and gazed past the front of the ship. The dark horizon had returned, but it wasn't a storm wall, it was ships. A whole fleet! Her mouth dropped open in shock. "Can we see their colors?"

Shaking his head, he shouted. "The rain is too heavy."

She wiped the rain from her lips and brushed them in thought. Her dark eyes peered through the storm, and the same instinct that drove her into the storm said to keep going. "Stay the course, Monsieur LeGalt."

Jean-Pierre gripped the wheel and replied, "Aye, Aye Captain."

Jeaneau could not tear her eyes away from the horizon, pondering what she was sailing them into. Frustrated, she fumbled for her pocket eyeglass, but could not find it in her drenched skirts.

Olav stepped next to her and handed her the ship's glass. She attempted to look through it, but it was wet. Grunting, she wiped the lens and looked again, but the rain obscured any clarity. The ships were blurred objects bobbing in the waves. She followed the sails upwards hoping to see some color. The flag whipped in the wind, but she saw them. "Blue... red...white."

"English or maybe us. Is it orange or red?" Olav asked.

Her brow furrowed. "I can't tell."

Glancing over her shoulder, her scarf whipped around and across her face, She spat and tore it away. The distance between them and the other ship grew, but it was still faring well in the storm. She looked at them through the glass and could see them also looking at the wall of ships. "Come on..." she whispered. "Break off."

The Tugas's ship heard her whisper and began to veer, pulling away.

A smile broke across her face. "They are breaking off!"

"Good," shouted Jean-Pierre, "but now we are still heading toward the fleet."

"Then pull away."

"There's a problem with that."

"What?"

"Captain," Olav began, "if a ship was heading straight for you with cannons primed and then pulled alongside...what would you think?"

"But we don't actually have cannons!"

"They don't know that."

"Oh, Hell!" She rushed to the edge of the quarterdeck and yelled, "Raise the white flag!"

NINE

Sitting on a Powder Keg

Commander-in-Cheif Arthur Herbert put down his glass and scratched under his hat.

The sailor who had given him the device nodded and said, "See. It's like I said, sir."

On the port side of the ship, deep into the storm they were skirting, was a ship tearing through the waves and heading straight for them. Her sails were simultaneously tacking to catch the wind while also fighting not to put too much force on the masts. Whoever was sailing this ship knew it well.

Arthur kept an eye on the ship as he passed information down the fleet ready to send alerts for defense. He found it highly unlikely that a sole ship would barrel through a storm to attack a fleet, but pirates were bold creatures.

Captain Roger Edevane stood on his own ship and studied the approaching ship. The rain blurred any distinctive markings, so the only thing he could determine was that it was of notable size with at least 3 masts and riding at an angle in an effort to cut through the storm quickly and deliberately.

He took the message from his bosun, and he confirmed his summation. He also knew that the current trajectory of the ship would have it cutting through his ship if it didn't turn. "Prep the cannons." His bosun nodded and scurried away, leaving him to watch.

The ship continued to draw closer, and the next message indicated that there might be two ships. Roger rubbed his chin and drew up his glass. He could see sailors scrambling across the deck. Some were tacking sail, but others were occupied on the deck, loading guns.

He shouted a message, to be passed to Arthur, of his findings and then looked again. Amidst the sailors, he saw a flutter of something familiar. Unsure, he wiped the water from the lens and looked again. There it was. Skirts. He followed the skirts up and saw a distinct brilliant blue coat and head wrapped in scarves. "Captain Elricksen?"

He leapt from the quarterdeck and towards the flag signaler, then paused, unsure how to signal Arthur. "Message the Admiral's ship that the approaching ship is friendly."

"Friendly, Captain?"

"Ally!" he boomed.

"Aye, Captain!"

Edevane lifted his glass again and watched the ship approach. From his brief time on the Daughter's Fortune, he did not find Jeaneau to be reckless with her ship, so there had to be a reason she would drive her vessel and cargo into a storm that could have been easily avoided. He drew his gaze to the ship behind her. It was smaller and struggling in the storm, and the rain blurred any chance to see its colors. "Relay the first ship is under distress."

*A*rthur reviewed the incoming signals which were always rudimentary in form, so left much to interpretation. All he knew was, unlike all his other captains, Edevane was declaring the ship an ally and under distress. He examined the ship through his glass and studied its markings. The ship seemed familiar, but he could not be certain.

"Admiral, the fleet is prepared to defend at your command."

*E*devane stood on his own ship and felt his stomach knot up with fear. "Signal."

The Daughter's Fortune was almost on them, and if she did not signal distress soon, the other ships would be forced to fire upon her.

Her ship was beginning to turn, but no flag was shown. His own bosun declared they were being told to aim. "Now Jeaneau!" he whispered.

Then there it was! Flying high from the mast, the white flag.

"Hold your fire!" he bellowed. "Tell the others!"

$\mathcal{O}$nce officially seen as in distress, Jean-Pierre slowly turned the Daughter's Fortune parallel with the fleet.

Signal flags flashed between the ships. The ship's colors were Dutch, so Jeaneau agreed to sail alongside until the storm broke.

During that time, the crew of Daughter's Fortune began to noticed the large number of militia on the other ships and Jeaneau noted many of the ships were members of the VOC. She had another sailor relieve Jean-Pierre from the helm and pulled him to her quarters. Olav entered and found them going over the charts.

"If this was our location before the Tugas and then we changed course into the storm, that puts us here." She stared at them both. "Why are there VOC with doubled Militia heading toward England?"

"Perhaps they are merely sailing through the channel on a greater expedition south," Olav conjectured.

"This late in the season?"

Crossing his arms, Jean-Pierre countered. "It's only October."

Jeaneau pressed, certain something was amiss. "And the winter storms have already begun."

$\mathcal{A}$rthur let out his own sigh of relief when he saw the white flag go up. The second ship retreated, and he could see the first was the Daughter's Fortune, now running parallel. He signaled for his own ship to pull to the port side of the vessel and box it into the fleet.

*J*eaneau came up top to discover Dutch ships on both sides and was not pleased. Both ships were requesting to board. She looked to her port side and saw an English Officer commanding the position of Fleet Admiral. On her starboard side, another English Officer held the helm. The captain took off his hat and she gawked. It was the sailor, Roger Smith.

She had merely a moment to process this when Jean-Pierre stated, "The Admiral requests permission to board."

She knew the request was only a formality, and was curious to know why the English were commanding Dutch ships. Signaling permission, she was unsure if she had actually escaped a worse fate than her present situation.

They attempted to lay boarding planks between moving vessels. While there was a finesse to two ships maintaining course and speed to pull off such a feat, it was rather comical watching poor sailors hold and adjust boards that the Admiral could cross. Jeaneau would have simply swung across on a rope, but apparently, the Admiral may have lacked that agility or simply desired the pomp and circumstance that came with trying to cross a plank at sea.

Jeaneau watched the delicate dance until she heard a call from behind. Turning she found Edevane waving.

"Ahoy, Captain!" he said, unable to hide the smile from his face.

"Ahoy!" she shouted, finding herself returning the smile.

"Permission to come aboard!"

"Granted. Do you wish for the boarding plank?"

"No need," he replied, and grabbed a rope, swinging onto her ship with practiced ease. His feet landed on her deck with surety, and he bowed. "Captain Elricksen."

She found herself grinning at his politeness. "Captain Smith?"

"Edevane. Captain Roger Edevane."

"Excellent, Edevane. You made it aboard," said a familiar voice.

Jeaneau turned and found Rafe standing on her ship. "Rafe?! What are you doing here?"

"I'm on company business. The more interesting question is what you are doing here." He stepped close to her and played with her sopping headscarf. "Mademoiselle, you look a fright."

She pushed his hand away. "I just traversed a storm. I am a bit wet."

Having successfully crossed the plank, Arthur approached.

Jeaneau faced the Admiral and nodded politely. She was about to speak, but something about his face stopped her. She studied him more closely. "Do I know you? I do know you…"

"Yes, you know me," he replied.

She stared more intently, then snatched the hat from his head. "Old Smith?"

Arthur's entourage balked at her brash action, but he laughed. "Yes, Captain."

Many of her crew stopped in their duties and watched the interaction, curious if they needed to respond.

"Perhaps we need to speak…privately," Edevane offered.

Jeaneau thrust Arthur's hat back into his chest and walked to her quarters, expecting the others to follow.

She knew not all of them could fit into her space, so once the shuffle of bodies was done, it was Arthur, Edevane, Jeaneau, Olav, Jean-Pierre and Rafe.

The door was barely shut before Jeaneau blurted, "Why are two former seamen of my crew now brandishing English colors and sailing Dutch ships toward English shores? The last I checked, James is King and Prince William is merely a Stadtholder. Has that changed?"

"You were right, Rafe. She is quick." Arthur brandished a broad beguiling smile.

"Captain Elricksen," Rafe cooed, "I'm afraid what we are doing is something of a politically delicate nature."

She scoffed. "Whatever the nature of this jaunt across the water, I am sure I want none of it. I'm also wet and tired and would like to move along. So though I permitted you on board out of politeness, I would like to get back on course."

"I'm afraid our plans will require me to take temporary confiscation of your ship," Arthur stated.

"You most certainly will not!"

"I truly wish it was not the case, Jeaneau," Rafe began, "but we are the spearhead of a rebellion, and you have accidentally come across our coup."

"What are you going on about?"

Jean-Pierre folded his arms and grimly replied, "I believe your Orange Prince is about to become their English King."

"Good Lord!" she declared.

"Now originally, you would have never known your part," said Arthur.

"My part!" she exclaimed. "I have nothing to do with this."

"Well…" Rafe interjected, "You were the ship that carried the letter asking the Orange Prince to overthrow King James."

"What?" She looked directly at Roger. His posture remained erect, but his eyes held regret. She turned, narrowing her gaze on the Arthur. "You used my ship."

"Your ship's role in all of this would have been unknown, but now that you have sailed into our fleet I have no choice but to keep you with us until we reach our destination."

"Let us go. I have no reason to expose your treason."

Olav sucked air through his teeth.

Jean-Pierre winced as he muttered, "Bad choice of words, Captain."

Arthur scratched his chin and softly replied, "It is only treason if we fail."

"And what if you fail? What about my ship then? My crew and I will be hanged, despite our innocence."

"I can't risk the future of an entire country for one ship."

"Politicians," she softly spat.

"Captain Elricksen," Arthur sternly spoke, "I suggest you use that intelligence and diplomacy I saw you wield in that salon right at this moment."

Not completely sure what he was talking about, she drew her eyes around the room. All men. Though Jean-Pierre and Olav would stand behind her decision, they were both clearly wanting her to remain calm and not act brashly. All expected her to yield. She was outnumbered both in the room and on the water. Her only choice was to do what they wanted.

She relented. "Very well then."

"Good decision, Captain. I will board militia onto your ship for protection."

"No, I will not have militia on this ship."

"If we go into battle, you will need able men to fight and protect your ship."

"I assure you. I will!"

"Jeaneau," Rafe implored.

"No," she snapped. "I have relented to the hostage of my ship, but it is my ship. I will sail it and my sailors will fight if it comes to it."

"How will I know you can defend this ship or yourself? Are you able?" Arthur inquired.

She pulled the wet scarf from her head, letting it hit the floor with a heavy thwap and calmly replied, "I am just as able as any to defend myself. If you wish a test of such, then I am willing to prove so."

"Lord Admiral," Edevane finally said. "I do not think we need…"

"No, Captain Edevane, if this woman wishes to lead a ship

in my fleet, I must know she and her sailors can do so. Your terms, Captain Elricksen."

"Pick a man and I will fight him."

Arthur smirked. He knew she was an able-bodied sailor, but a fighter? "Excellent. Edevane, you will do the honor."

Without hesitation he replied, "I respectfully refuse."

"You respectfully refuse?!" Arthur bellowed.

"Out of respect for Captain Elricksen, I cannot engage in such an interaction."

Jeaneau's eyes flared with fury. "Do you think I cannot fight? Do you think I am weak?"

"No, Captain. Quite the opposite." He met her gaze. "I do not question your strength or your ability to defend your ship. Therefore, I see no reason for you to prove it."

She stared at him for a long moment then only replied, "Oh."

"Nonetheless," Arthur stated, "It is not whether you question her strength, but whether I do." He stepped over and opened the door. "We will have Lt. Samuels test your mettle."

"As you wish," Jeaneau replied and stepped out the door.

Fight Like a Girl

On the main deck of the Daughter's Fortune, Jeaneau stood in the center of a fighter's circle, facing a man nearly matching her in height. He began to remove his coat, then hesitated.

She brandished a smile. "You can take off your coat for movement. It will not shock me."

Her opponent balked at her statement, unsure how to respond.

"If you feel that would put me at a disadvantage, I can take mine off as well."

There was a mixture of murmurs and chuckles among the watching crowd.

Olav was standing next to Arthur and Roger. He snorted softly then said, "You know she was raised on a ship. Her whole family. Father, Mother, and her brother."

Jeaneau's opponent, Lt Samuels, finally took off his coat and rolled his shoulders. He clearly had trepidations about fighting her, but he would not let that stop him. They were both handed rapiers.

Arthur said, "This is merely a matter of mettle, so no stabbing. Flat of blade only, gentleman…and lady."

Jeaneau did not take off her jacket and moved into a fighting stance, revealing that her coat was slit at the arms to allow for a fuller range of movement. She waited for the attack.

Samuels moved into position, then lunged.

She parried the strike and stepped back.

He lunged again.

She parried and moved again.

Olav continued, "When she was about 10 you couldn't tell the difference between her and her brother. They were both long and lanky and often would trick the sailors into thinking one was the other. They were both very curious, and by that time, knew every inch of the ship. You could easily see they both would grow up to be excellent sailors. One day their mother came out of her quarters and found a seaman teaching them to fight."

Samuels continued to strike and Jeaneau continued to parry but had not yet attacked. He glanced at his commander a bit baffled, but Arthur motioned for him to continue.

"Her mother was livid, and right there on the deck, laid into the sailor for teaching a girl how to fight."

Jeaneau shifted her stance, but the movement was obscured by her skirts, so when Samuels attempted to strike again she parried and spun out of the way, leaving his flank open, allowing her to slap her blade up against his side.

He jumped back in shock, and Jeaneau's crew let out a joyful shout.

"Her father shows up and her mother starts yelling at him and tells him, 'You can teach our son, but no daughter of mine will learn how to fight!'"

Jeaneau moved into offense and Samuels found himself challenged.

He parried most of her blows, realizing she was an actual opponent, he began to truly fight her.

The duel quickly turned into an even match, and he finally landed a few strikes of his own. His sword struck against her back, but instead of hitting cloth and flesh, the surface was hard like wood.

This caused him to pause momentarily, allowing Jeaneau to get in another strike and regain her stance.

"Her father looked at her mother and said, 'You are right. I will not teach my daughter how to fight like a man.' Her mother looked so proud she had won the argument. Jeaneau was devastated by these words. She looked so sad and broken until her father then grinned broadly and said with a sparkle in his eye, 'Jeaneau this world is run by men, and they will always see you as less than them. So I will not teach you how to fight like a man. I will teach you how to fight dirty.'"

Edevane glanced at Olav, who responded with a knowing grin and gestured for him to keep watching.

Jeaneau allowed the unsteady Samuels to lunge at her again, but instead of stepping back, she moved into attack. He responded quickly, thinking she had made a fatal error, grabbed her from behind, and pressed her up against him.

Feeling victorious, he tightened his hold. "Do you yield?"

Jeaneau smiled as she moved her feet into position. Samuels assumed she was merely struggling and did not realize her skirts were tangling around his legs.

He asked again, "Do you yield?"

She elbowed him in the chest and all the air left his lungs. His grip slackened allowing her to slam her foot down onto his and spin around, tightening her skirts around his legs. She grabbed the fabric and pulled violently, lifting his feet off the ground, sending him down on his back.

She rushed his prone body and stepped firmly on his chest. Samuels was still trying to draw in air when she put her sword under his chin and asked, "Do you yield?"

The deck of the ship exploded with roaring cheers.

Arthur smiled broadly and shouted, "Fair nuff, Captain Elricksen. The ship is yours."

She put out a hand to Samuels and helped him up, then looked at the Arthur. "This ship has always been mine and no one will take it from me." Her eyes moved to Rafe. "Ever."

ELEVEN

Sitting on a Powder Keg

The men moved to set the boarding plank once again between the two ships, and Jeaneau stood next to it waiting to bid her unwanted guests farewell. Arthur scratched his nose and looked at this bold woman. Her hair, though in a tight braid, was a frizzled mess from the rain and fight. She wore a look upon her face that carried a defiance only brought on by years of fighting assumptions she did not believe in, and she fought them well.

Yet in that same moment, a coquettish grin blended with her determined look as she spoke softly, "Admiral, I believe I have proved my mettle, and so I respectfully request that you release my ship and let us continue on our own passage."

He smiled at her charm and found her demeanor quite exhilarating, but the fate of England was in his hands, and he would not let the smile of a woman deter him. "I, unfortunately, cannot, and as requested, I will not put militia on your ship, but a few of my men must stay."

"We do not have the room or accommodations to support additional men on this ship. I could not possibly feed or board them."

"I would be happy to stay upon the ship as a liaison,

Admiral." Rafe interjected. "I know Jeaneau, and I am but one man. Surely she can accommodate one."

Jeaneau stiffened slightly at this prospect but did not show her inner distaste to the suggestion.

"No, Rafe," Arthur replied. "You are my liaison."

"Perhaps, Admiral," Roger intervened, "I can send men in shifts to monitor the ship. This will require her ship to sail near mine, and the men can move back and forth. This will allow the men the proper time to rest and recuperate and not put any further stress on Captain Elricksen's food supply."

Arthur mulled over the suggestion and then nodded in approval. He looked at Jeaneau, "Do you agree to these terms, Captain?" He could clearly see that she did not.

She slowly nodded. "Very well, I agree to these terms, but under protest."

"I would expect nothing less, Captain." The Lord Admiral tugged on his coat and moved onto the plank. "Captain Edevane, I will leave you to secure and monitor this ship until we reach our destination."

"Yes, Admiral."

"Come along, Rafe. I have reports to check from the other ships."

Rafe stepped up to Jeaneau. "Jeaneau, you never fail to entertain, but I much rather prefer our other encounters." He bowed and took her hand into his. "As always it has been a pleasure, Captain." He kissed it softly and then winked at her.

She smiled back politely hiding her inner rage at his inappropriate comment. Her cheeks flushing and fingers flinching, she fought the need to lash out at him either verbally or physically. In a cold tone, she replied, "Goodbye, Rafe."

Tensing, realizing the finality of her words, he prepared to retort.

"Rafe!" Arthur bellowed. "Woo the lass on your own time."

*J*eaneau's hand balled up into a fist, but she remained still and collected. She had won the right to captain her ship and would not threaten her small victory because of a few demeaning comments.

As the last of Lord Admiral's entourage exited her ship, she walked towards her quarters, leaving the crew to remove the plank and set the ship to once again sail. She could feel her anger swelling inside and needed to be away from everyone. She would not further her humiliation by losing her temper.

Edevane stepped toward her but found a hand on his chest. It was Olav.

"Let her cool off, or you may find yourself an unintended victim."

Edevane stopped and nodded. "I will see to creating the rotation schedule." He grabbed a rope, stepped up to the railing, and paused to look back at the captain's quarters one last time before he swung back to his ship.

Jean-Pierre stepped next to Olav. "That Lord Admiral is a bit of a pompous ass, but I'm starting to like Young Smith."

Olav scratched his chin. "I think Jeaneau would agree with that opinion."

Jean-Pierre rubbed his temple softly. "I know…"

*E*mmet burst into Jeaneau's quarters, his arms filled with food.

Jeaneau was changing out of her wet clothes and her

hardened pair of bodies. She showed no surprise to Emmet's entrance and was still clearly fuming.

Emmet dropped the food on the table and went over to the small cask in the corner of the room. He opened its spout and drew out two glasses of wine.

Half-dressed, Jeaneau took the offered cup, downed it quickly, then plopped into her chair. They did not speak for a long time, simply eating and drinking until Emmet could see Jeaneau's eyes soften, and her body relax.

Finally, Emmet spoke. "Brilliant fight."

Jeaneau snorted, "Hooray."

"No seriously, who knew skirts could be an advantage in a fight. I might just start wearing them."

Jeaneau let out a full-bodied laugh. "That would be a sight."

"What? I have worn skirts before. I just prefer the freedom of trousers."

"I find skirts quite comfortable," Jeaneau said and took another sip.

"Don't they get in the way? Not sure how you manage rigging with all those layers flapping about."

"True, it's something you learn, and I do prefer having the slit in my skirts so I can move, despite my mother's misgivings."

"It's also disarming when you fight. I couldn't see your footing, which made it hard to tell whether you were moving back or forth."

"I know. I use that to my advantage. You'd also be surprised how many blows from a sword you can avoid because they get stopped or tangled by skirts." She sipped again and rubbed her eyes.

The weariness of the day was finally settling in. She had not rested or eaten since the Tugas began chasing them, and now that the adrenaline was leaving, she felt extremely tired. Even though her ship was not completely out of danger, she conceded to herself that she could close her eyes for a moment.

Emmet watched her eyes droop close a few times before finally remaining shut. Jeaneau's hand slackened around the glass, and Emmet caught it before it tumbled on the floor. He stood and collected up the food, so the rats would not come scurrying in, and left her asleep in the chair.

*H*ours later, Jeaneau woke refreshed, but quickly found sore muscles when she attempted to move from her strange sleeping position. She stood and stretched. She could tell that the sun had set, which meant she had missed her duties on the night shift, so she drew on her coat and stepped top side to see the status of the ship. Dread quickly washed over her when she remembered that her vessel was being held hostage, which meant there would be soldiers aboard.

Nonetheless, she opened the door and stepped onto the deck. There she found her ship running smoothly. She saw one soldier standing at the prow of the ship and turned to look for the other. Roger was at the aft. She wanted to be angry at the current status of her ship but found his presence more calming than agitating. She walked up to the quarter-deck, greeted the sailor at the helm, and then nodded to Roger with a polite grin. "Captain."

He slowly turned and began to bow but stopped midway noticing that she was standing in her coat and chemise. The moonlight cut through the gauzy fabric giving him a glimpse of her legs underneath. He completely dropped his head to block his view then as he rose, he kept his eyes on her face, "Captain Elricksen. Did you sleep well?"

"Too well. I missed my duties."

"Yes, once it was clear you were still sleeping and needed the rest, I offered my services to Jean-Pierre. I felt that it was the least I could do."

She stiffened slightly, but remained polite as she said, "I thank you for your services, but my needs are no greater than those of my crew and I am sure they all need rest, no reason for me to receive special consideration."

"Then consider it a way for you to provide the same service to your men. Now that you have rested, they can also begin to recover."

She crossed her arms. "Are you always so polite?"

"I am as polite as the situation dictates."

"How does one so polite ever achieve anything in the military?"

"One can have a force of will and still be civil. You have shown that yourself."

She blinked. "I have?"

He nodded. "When the Admiral confiscated your ship, you negotiated terms rather than attack. When both Rafe and the Admiral insulted you, you did not retaliate because to do so would have been impolite."

"No, I did not respond because it was not advantageous to react at that moment. If given the opportunity…"

"Now Captain, I must stop you there. I cannot have you speak of the Admiral in a disparaging manner, no matter what actions he took against you."

"Why not?"

"Because even when I do not agree with his actions, he is my commander, and I must comply."

"Well, I certainly could not. And here I thought all the respect you had for Old Smith was that of a son to his father," she said, then processed his words. "Wait, you do not agree with the Admiral?"

"I did not say I presently disagree with him."

"So do you?"

"To say I disagree with the Lord Admiral's actions would be a punishable action, but if I were given the choice…" He drew his eyes to hers. "I would have done things differently."

She grinned. "Perhaps someday when you are an Admiral, you will have that chance."

"Your compliment is noted, but I doubt I will ever achieve such a rank."

She arched her brow. "Why not?"

"Because I am not of noble birth."

"Oh?" she said with honest surprise.

"No, at least not legitimately."

"Oh!" Jeaneau softly exclaimed at the revelation that he was a bastard. "But someone paid for your commission into the military?"

"He did," Roger replied.

"Out of love or obligation?" she boldly asked.

"I like to think it's both."

"Well, at least there is that."

"Yes."

She rubbed her arms softly, warding off the chill in the air, and gazed over the water and ships. Reluctantly, she did find a sense of security in sailing with other vessels.

*R*oger studied her in the silence. Her hair was free of braids and scarves allowing tendrils to dance wildly in the wind. It was unruly and shined even in the dimness of the moonlight. Her skin was shockingly white for someone living at sea, but he assumed this was a result of her own rigorous regime to keep it from burning. This also made him wonder about her age. At 23 he was already tan and weathered from the sea, but her skin showed little sign of the elements.

He once again pondered her role as captain of a merchant ship and asked, "Why have you not joined the VOC?"

His question took her off guard. She studied him for a moment, trying to read the intention of his query. She sighed and replied, "Because I see no need to join."

"But like our own East India Trading, does it not offer security in the form of insurance over losses and protection on the seas?"

"Insurances are for investors, not sailors. We take the risks and I see no need for additional men on my ship whose only duty is to protect it in case of attack. I fight my own battles."

"As you have proven." He paused then said, "But when you were attacked by pirates, you had to flee and drive your ship into a storm. Very risky move."

"When you are seen as weaker than others you must take greater risks to prove your opponent wrong."

"Like in your fight with Lt Samuels?"

"Pardon?"

"You first disarmed him with propriety, then you held a defensive position until you understood his fighting style. You even allowed yourself to be struck to open up an attack of opportunity. Then once you were ready to defeat him, you made him think he had won, so you could administer your final blow. And may I say how comical Samuels looked, as his feet flew up into the air."

Soft laughter fluttered from her throat. "The goal of any combat is to knock your opponent off balance. Whether that be forcing them to take their ship into dangerous water, or beguiling a man into thinking he has the advantage."

"That explains the ballroom as well," he said, unaware that all his inner contemplations were flying out at once.

"The ballroom?" she asked.

"Social encounters. The day we left your ship, I saw you

that night at a social engagement. I apologize that I did not make myself known, but…"

A smile broke across her face. "Too busy planning a coup?"

He nodded reluctantly. "Yes." He shifted slightly and steered the topic aft. "I suspect anytime you are in public and on land, you beguile the men around you."

"Well," she pondered, moving closer to him, "My mother says the secret to men is making them think they are in charge."

"When you are on your ship, you stand tall and sure to ensure their respect. You hold a man's eye, and your voice is firm. Yet, when you are at a party, you sit instead, so that men can stand over you, thinking they have the advantage."

"Exactly." She grinned.

He continued, "When you are on a ship you dress for utility and means, but on land you cover yourself in frivolous silks and lace to imbue your femininity."

She stepped even closer. "Men tend to like pretty things."

He tilted his head down slightly. "So you are a coquette."

Her jaw had slackened slightly, and she was staring at him with shock and alarm. Face flushed, she stammered, "Did you just call me a coquette? A shallow, pretty thing that seeks men who shower them with attention and wealth. I am unsure which unnerves me more, that you speak so frankly, or how well you deluded my well-groomed tactics into one malicious word!"

He straightened his posture. "Have I said something out of turn?"

Her mouth opened and closed a few times as she worked to find words, then she said, "I am not a coquette."

"I did not mean to infer…" he began.

"Every action is chosen with great contemplation. My clothes for the seas or land serve a purpose."

"Which is what I said."

"No, you said my dresses were frivolous. Even the colors have intention. You called me a coquette. I promise you, good sir, that finding myself a wealthy husband is the last thing I wish to do!"

He saw her feet shift into a sturdier stance. She was upset with his words and ready to defend herself. He knew he could either allow her to attack or squelch the fire which he had unintentionally started.

"Then what is your purpose at those parties?"

"Contracts. Strictly business. If a man wishes to think otherwise, that is his folly."

"Certainly, but what if others misconstrue your intentions and attempt to take advantage?"

"Then just like Lt. Samuels, they would quickly find themselves with a blade to their throat."

"No quarter given then?"

"Only if I choose to do so."

Roger straightened his stance and took a step back from her. "My apologies for such curt words. I clearly see what I mistook as frivolity in that ballroom is simply the same tactics you used on Samuels. Lure them in, then take them out when they least expect it."

"Fighting or Politics, that is the end game."

He felt a mixture of tension and vulnerability between them. Bowing, he replied. "I understand. Again, my apologies. It was simply an observation."

She nodded, but surprised that he relented rather than fight. "Well...you took me a bit off guard."

"Evidently, but my remarks remain true. You do think out your actions."

"Yes...I find I must."

"Just as you would plot a course at sea knowing exactly how far you can sail on the soundness of your ship and crew."

"Yes," she replied. "Glad to see someone understands my actions."

"I commend your tactics at sea, it is clear you know her well, but fear your tactics on land are more perilous."

"Oh?"

"I worry there are more monsters in the seas of humanity than in all the oceans."

"I quite agree, but we must risk the monsters in order to reap our rewards."

He stood silent for a moment mulling over her words. "What rewards do you seek?"

She ran her fingers slowly through her hair, letting the last tendrils slip through her fingers as she said, "Whatever it takes to give me one more day at sea."

He shifted his feet and felt his throat tighten. Swallowing, he asked, "So your reward is not marriage?"

"Oh Good Lord No! Investors!"

"Investors?"

"Yes, just like the VOC or any other ship, I must have people willing to pay for us to ship their goods, and even more so, have those that wish to invest in our journey and then be rewarded in monetary means if we are successful."

Titlated by their conversation and curious, he inquired. "So you are still convincing men to give you things. Rather coquettish don't you think?"

"Why is it when a woman negotiates for money, she is called coquette, but when a man does it, it's called business?"

"Well, there is a business where women work for money," he said without thinking and quickly saw his error.

Her anger flared again. "Yes, there is. It's called working, whether cooking food, mending clothes, or exchanging… services and women do it every day. If they are lucky, they do get paid and as for the woman who does get paid for lying on her back, I respect her too. At least she gets something versus the woman bound into it by martial duties with nothing to show for it, but a pregnant belly and complete loss of freedom."

Roger swallowed and stood at attention. Moving back, he bowed deeply, keeping his head hung low, and said, "Captain Elricksen, my apologies for such crass remarks. My tongue is looser than decorum dictates. It was spoken of without thinking and unnecessary." He straightened back up and looked at her directly. "Allow me to recuse myself. I will send over the next guards." He waited for any semblance of a nod then stepped away.

*J*eaneau watched him leave in utter silence. As she watched him cross back over, he did so without turning to look at her. He was not requesting her forgiveness or making her feel guilty. He clearly declared he was wrong and that was that.

Jean-Pierre stepped next to her and asked, "Did I hear yelling? Is everything well?"

"Everything is…fine," she said in a disconnected tone. It only took another moment before she was pulled out of her daze and looked at Jean-Pierre. "The next set of marines are coming over. I am going to find something to eat."

"Find some clothes too, while you are at it."

She paused and looked down at her attire. She was still wearing just her coat and chemise. She spent an entire conversation with Roger in an inappropriate state and he never said a word.

If Rafe had seen her like this, there would have been three bawdy remarks and she was certain he would have groped her at least twice. She was sure even the Old Smith would have said something, but Roger spoke to her with ease, frankness, and propriety. Her fingers played across her lips as she pondered all of it.

"Jeaneau?" Jean-Pierre asked again, "Is everything well?"

She dropped her hand from her mouth and looked at her friend, "I…" She gazed past Jean-Pierre's shoulder and saw the silhouette of Captain Edevane on his ship. He stood tall, with his feet grounded, and oversaw the next Marines to cross to her ship. His eyes stayed focused on his task and did not drift in her direction. She huffed softly, "He…" She then put her hands on her hips and asked, "Do you think I am a coquette?"

Jean-Pierre was taking a sip from his mug when she asked this and proceeded to sputter and choked, "A coquette?"

"Yes, a frivolous, shallow damsel who uses her wiles to have men shower her with wealth and attention?"

He carefully wiped his mouth clean knowing he was in murky water and said, "Are you? No. Do you often act like one? Yes."

"But that's what men want! Men don't like strong women or tall women or smart women. They want them pale, and delicate, without an opinion of their own. And don't tell me they don't like the courting and vying for a woman's attention. How can they want these things, then label their ideal woman with such a derogatory name?"

"I don't know, Jeaneau. I wish I could say men are less confusing than women, but they are not." He stared at her. "Why are we talking about this? Did Young Smith call you a coquette?"

"Yes…no…I don't know."

He opened his palms toward her, gesturing for an explanation.

She scrunched her nose, huffed, and then finally gave a defeated groan. "I honestly don't know."

Jean-Pierre snorted softly. "I have not seen many who have left you baffled."

"I'm not baffled. One minute he was asking me a flurry of questions, the next complimenting my tactics and then he says coquettes are nothing but whores and then he just…leaves.”

"He called you a coquette and then a whore?” Jean-Pierre carefully asked.

"No…yes…wait, no. I’m…ugh!” She threw her hands in the air and spun around. "I’m going to change.”

TWELVE

En Garde

____

The next day proceeded without incident, but there was a discernable air of unease among the crew with the constant reminder that they were not free. As the English controlled Dutch Fleet sailed closer to its destination, many considered their options. Jeaneau knew she could not collect her sailors and speak to them as a group without creating suspicion. Carefully, she found them individually or in small groups and eased their fears.

She told them that if an opportunity presented itself, they would break from the fleet, but they would have to be patient. Storms and the mere size of the fleet were slowing their progress, but with each passing hour, they were playing part in an English coup.

"It is nearly Guy Fawkes's day," mentioned one of her sailors. "Be damn good timing if they land on the shore that day. Showing up, turning over a tyrannical king and taking back parliament."

As she worked her way through her crew, her eyes drifted to Roger's ship. She often found him doing similar tasks on his own vessel. He would speak with crew and marines, and he would also look over at her ship. His gaze was solemn and reposed, the look of a sailor doing his job. Jean-Pierre came to her side and caught her staring. Averting her eyes, she went back to securing a tie.

"You have eased the crew some, but what is the actual plan?"

"I'm unsure, but I know the opportunity will present itself." She replied, her hands setting the knots with practiced ease.

"We are running out of time."

Tugging on the rope, harder than necessary, she sighed, "I know."

"Actions must be taken."

"Violence is a last resort." She stated, heading to her next task.

Jean-Pierre followed, pressing the matter. "Perhaps you can find a way to distract them."

"It's not like I can throw a rock and run the other way," she quipped.

"Perhaps you can persuade a certain captain to look the other way? It's his ship and crew that are watching us."

"And exactly how do I persuade him?"

"Well…" he replied in an implicating tone.

Her head whipped sharply, and she looked at him aghast. "Are you suggesting I seduce him?"

He shrugged his shoulders nonchalantly. "A sailor uses all his skills to survive at sea. You have a skill most do not."

"We have discussed that Mr. Smith cannot be persuaded in such a manner. He is different."

"I don't care how different he is. He's still a man."

"Jean-Pierre, there are times when your advice baffles me. Sometimes you tell me to fight like a man and then you tell me to act like a woman."

"Because Jeaneau, unlike most people in this world, you can do both, so why not do so?"

*J*eaneau was in her quarters finishing her evening meal when she heard a knock. Rising from her chair, she opened the door and discovered Captain Roger Edevane on the other side. His manner was stiff with evident action to hide an inner unease.

"May I enter, Captain?"

She stepped to the side. "You may."

He ducked his head and stepped in. She hesitated for only a moment before closing the door. Sauntering back over to her table, she grabbed a second glass. "Libations, Captain?"

"No thank you."

"What brings you here? I did not think you'd be taking another shift."

"I have not. There are two men up top."

Her shoulders slumped at the mention of the marines, but then they rose again. She smiled politely. "Then please drink and eat with me."

He paused for a moment, before sitting and taking the cup.

The wine was good, quite good, and went well with the meal. They ate in polite silence for a time, allowing the action of eating together to ease the tension between them. If she was still offended by his previous comments, she showed no indication.

He wondered if bringing it up would be wise, but felt compelled to do so. "As for my comments the other night, I did not mean to imply your actions as a captain or woman are untoward…"

"Captain…Edevane, correct?"

He nodded.

"I am aware I am not like other women. I know that most

women who work in a man's world emulate men and with good reason. It makes men accept them more, never completely, but more. If I wished to do so, I could dress as a man and act like a man and live a much easier life, but I don't want to live in such deception nor do I feel I have to."

"I agree."

She blinked. "You do?"

"I do. No one should live in a world of deception to do what they want and are good at."

"Exactly."

"So why do you deceive men when you are on land?"

Mildly baffled, "I don't understand what you mean."

"Why do you put on airs when you are among people on land?"

A scowl drew across her face. "Captain, why do you keep bringing this up? You have only seen me on a ship?"

"I saw you in Amsterdam. After we landed. Large gathering. You were well attended to."

"I see."

"You just said you chose not to dress like a man to gain greater acceptance. Surely you could be yourself on land and still achieve what you want?"

"I am being myself, just a different part of me. I know what I must do to get the things I need. Not unlike you and your duties."

He furrowed his brow. "Pardon?"

"You know that it is unjust that my ship is being held captive. By your own indirect words you disagree with your Admiral's actions, but you still obey them, because you must. If you think it is any different for others merely because they haven't taken oaths, then you are mistaken."

She stabbed her meat and sawed through it with her knife. "People take silent oaths their whole lives. Now there are those that will break an oath at a moment's notice and others that would die before they would ever violate such promises, but," she stabbed the piece of meat and brandished it at him. "They exist nonetheless. I have a duty and obligation to this crew and my family to make sure our ships keep sailing and if that means putting on airs and wooing men then I will do that for as long as I can." She kept her eyes on him as she took the bite and chewed with determination.

"And then what?" He asked, keeping her gaze. "What happens when your wooing puts you in a place that you do not wish to be?"

She took a sip of wine and said, "Then like any good expert, I will use every tool at my disposal and I will find a way out."

"Then you consider…intimacy a tool."

She popped an olive into her mouth and grinned. "Absolutely."

He took a long sip of wine and mulled over her response. She watched his brow furrow again. He slowly picked up a piece of bread and took a bite. His eyes fixed on a spot on the table as he slowly chewed.

He drew up his eyes to her. "If intimacy is a weapon, what do you consider it in connection to love and marriage?"

His frankness caught her offgaurd. Carefully drawing in a breath, she said, "Marriage is merely a contract and sex an addendum."

"And love."

"Love has nothing to do with it."

"Love has nothing to do with marriage?"

"Certainly not. If there is love in marriage, then it's a happy accident."

"And love to sex?"

"Love and sex often get confused and muddled, but you can have one without the other."

She picked up the lip of her glass with her fingertips and before sipping asked, "Captain Edevane do you have conversations like this often?"

His posture straightened. "I…" He cleared his throat. "No."

She dropped her feet to the floor and leaned forward. "Then why me?"

"Because I feel I can ask you such questions without great offense."

She intently studied his face. "And why do you think that?"

"Because you have an honesty about you, despite your tendency to disguise your true self."

Batting her hand in frustration, she huffed, "There you go again assuming that I don't like dressing up and going to parties."

"Do you?"

"Yes! I like wearing pretty dresses and meeting new people. Perhaps not everything I'm expected to do, but the same goes for when I am at sea."

"What do you not enjoy doing at sea?"

Subconsciously, they had both drawn closer to each other, leaning over the table in candid discussion. She glanced down at the plate of food and moved it around a bit. "I do not like being a harsh captain, but there are times I must."

"Agreed, there are times for such difficult decisions."

Her gaze lifted to meet his. "Then you also understand that similar decisions are made on land too. I may not want to do them, but I must."

"I can see your point, but do not agree with it."

"Why is that?"

"I do not believe…intimacy is a tool."

"Why not?" She put her elbow on the table and leaned on her hand.

"I believe it is special and should be cherished and used wisely."

"A sword can be cherished, but it is still used."

"But a wise fighter does not draw his sword on another unless absolutely necessary."

Her fingers played with the rim of his cup. "Do you never duel merely for fun?"

He pulled the cup away and sipped softly. "Only with a practiced partner, someone who understands my skills and may challenge them without causing injury."

Their faces were so close the wine on his breath mingled between them, and he saw her pulse pound against her throat.

"So you've never dueled in the heat of the moment?"

"I have," he replied softly. "But there is always a price for such hasty actions." His eyes dropped to her lips. "Someone always gets hurt."

Her hand gripped her skirt. "So no foolish swordplay for you?"

"No," he said, pulling himself away and leaning back into his chair. "My sword will stay sheathed until needed."

She leaned back and drank deep from her cup, slaking her thirst. Looking over her glass, she studied him in deep contemplation. As her fingers brushed her lips, she licked the tip of one and asked, "Your fleet plans to land on Guy Fawkes's day."

Edevane's eyes bulged slightly, but he replied, "I was unaware you knew of the day, but yes."

"We have less than twenty-four hours til then. What is the Admiral's plan for our ship?"

"His plan is to have you within the back end of the fleet, and once the engagement is successful, to relinquish your ship if possible."

"If possible. Do you truly believe he will just let us go?"

Roger tugged at his coat and replied, "No."

She shoved her plate softly in frustration. "Then what does that mean for us."

"I assume that he will demand your loyalty and submission into his fleet, and when you refuse, declare your ship as bounty during the naval action and hand it over to the VOC for fair trade."

Thrusting herself from her seat, she shouted. "He can't do that."

"He can."

She walked over to the window and gazed outside. Her rush to the window appeared rash, but it was intentional. Next to the window was her rapier, which she grabbed, using the fullness of her skirts to obscure the action. She stood still for a moment. "I won't let him."

Roger empathized with her situation and knew this was one of those moments she would choose to be cruel. Before he could say anything further, she spun around and thrust the rapier in his direction.

He quickly stood in defense but was not fast enough and found the tip of her blade at his throat.

"You will remove your men from my ship."

He stared at her in pleasant surprise. "That was the plan."

Her brow crinkled. "What was that?"

He lifted his hands to show he relented and said, "The plan. I came on board to oversee the changing of shift and before the new marines come on board you are to push me from the ship and escape."

She looked at him in disbelief. "I'm to…wait, you're helping?"

He nodded. "My ship is instructed to stay with yours. I've already noticed that you have slowly slipped to the back of the fleet. If I am correct your plan is to disrupt the changing of the guard and escape."

She lowered her sword. "Why am I pushing you overboard?"

"How else can I explain your escape? Plus, my men will be too busy rescuing me to pursue."

"Why not simply come with me?"

"Because as you said, I have an oath."

"Are you not breaking it?"

"Only if you were a threat to the fleet or the mission, which I have never believed you to be."

His intent softened her face, but independent resolve caused her to raise the sword again. "At this point, I can keep you as my own hostage and still succeed."

"But at what price? Keep me and they must pursue. Let me go and you are no threat unless you make yourself one."

She held the rapier at his throat a moment longer before lowering it again and replying, "Fair enough. Care to enact my escape?"

Bowing his head, he consented. "On your command."

THIRTEEN

Man Overboard

Roger stepped onto the main deck and ordered his men to return. They seemed confused by the early exchange but did not question their commanding officer. Once they had crossed, there was a discussion on the other ship to collect the next shift of marines.

Roger turned to Jeaneau. "Now is your chance. Push me in."

"The water is freezing," she hissed, "and you will surely drown in that coat."

He pulled off his sword and coat dropping them at her feet in an intentionally dramatic fashion. "Then brandish that weapon of yours and force me to jump. I am unencumbered and will survive until my crew can rescue me."

She lifted her rapier and pointed it at him. "That is a great risk."

"One I am willing to take…for a friend." He backed up on the railing.

She found her heart in her throat and her hand slicking with sweat.

He steadied his feet, held her eyes, and smiled. "Do know,

I find you to be a fine captain." Still smiling, he jumped backward into the water.

Jeaneau dropped her sword arm and quickly ran to the railing. She saw him hit the water and quickly rush behind them. Cries of alarm sounded from both ships.

Jeaneau turned and found her night crew staring in confusion awaiting orders. "All hands on deck! Change course, open all sails, and pull as far from the fleet as quickly as possible."

Her crew immediately scrambled to their posts and the rest began to spill out from below.

As the ship changed course and gained speed, she found herself watching the fleet. The main body of ships were still maintaining course, but Roger's ship had dropped anchor and boats were in the water. She feared his ship was going too fast for a timely rescue but could see dimly lit torches bobbing up and down on the waves as they searched for him. She reached down, picking up his sword and coat. It was still warm.

Jean-Pierre bounded up to her. Though alert, it was clear he had woken from sleep and was a disheveled mess. "What the hell did I miss?" he asked. "How did we get away from the fleet?"

She hefted the coat over her arm and looked at her first mate. "By the actions of one Mr. Smith."

*R*oger bobbed in the water, watching all known life swiftly sail away from his position. The cold waters sunk into his bones. To keep his circulation moving, he began to swim towards his ship. He knew the dangers of jumping into the water and had already formed a plan to keep himself alive till the boats arrived.

However, plans often have trouble with reality. He knew he needed to keep swimming or treading water to keep himself afloat and warm, but if he swam too fast or fought to keep his head above the water, his reserve energy would rapidly deplete.

What he did not account for was the violent involuntary shaking, which impeded his steady movements and his ability to take in large amounts of air. Then in protest, a cramp formed in his leg, sending searing pain through his body. He gasped again and found both swimming and treading water nearly impossible.

He looked for the rescue ships, but disorientation was beginning to set in. He stopped swimming because he did not know which direction to go. His only instinct now was to keep his head above water.

Waves started to lap and roll over his head and his only thoughts boiled down to breathe and head above water.

Breathe.

He tried to move his limbs, but they seemed to fight his every command.

Breathe.

He choked and spat out water.

Breathe air.

Suddenly, he felt great pressure on his arm and something pulling him. He instinctively fought the action thinking he was sinking, but the force pulled against him and then he felt his back land against solid ground.

His lungs desperately scraped in air, and it took a moment before his gasping for air slowed and he could focus on his surroundings. He was on one of the small boats and men were shouting and waving torches. One man pulled viciously at the oars propelling the boat back to the ship.

By the time the boat abutted the ship, Roger was wrapped in another man's coat, shaking violently from the cold. He tried to climb the rope ladder, but his muscles were too weak and unstable. He felt men hauling and pushing him up the ladder. One man squeezed his hand around the rope, and another placed his foot on a rung. Then someone removed one hand from the rope and placed it higher up.

He attempted to help but found his actions inadequate. Nevertheless, they were successful in getting him onto the deck where his knees gave out, and he fell in a crumpled heap.

His mind could not understand why his body was so weak but he was out of the water and should be safe. He could breathe, but so cold that even drawing in air seemed hard and unnecessary. His thoughts began to drift, then there was only blackness.

Jeaneau thrust Roger's coat onto her own chest and poured another glass of wine. She was finishing it off when Olav came in.

"We have pulled away from the fleet and they do not appear to be following. Well done, Captain."

She grunted softly and poured another glass.

"So what did you do to convince the boy to help?"

She gestured with the cup. "He merely offered his assistance."

"So you didn't have to…persuade him?"

She slammed her cup onto the table. "What is it with you and Jean-Pierre? I thought you respected me more as a captain?"

"We don't?" he asked, confused.

"Both you and Jean-Pierre think I must constantly use my feminine wiles to get what I want. I run this ship as a captain, not as a woman."

"But you are still a woman, so why not use it?"

She shouted into the sky and then glared at him. "Because of thoughts like that. I would love to be my whole self all the time, but the rest of the world has a different opinion on what a woman can and cannot be. A woman can have influence over men without seducing him. Sex is not the only form of persuasion!" She poured another glass and continued to drink with abandon.

Jean-Pierre and Lance had arrived by this point and looked at Olav, who appeared confused and lost.

"Captain," Jean-Pierre said, intentionally using her title. "We respect you and know that you will do whatever it takes to protect this ship and us. Forgive us if we recommended an action that you disfavor."

She groaned softly. "I don't disfavor the act of seduction, just don't assume it's my first course of action."

"Acknowledged," Jean-Pierre replied.

Jeaneau slumped into her chair and sipped once more.

"We have escaped. Why do you still appear upset?"

Lance stared at the two other men and gawked. "She just forced a man into the drink. A man that we know, and you wonder why she is upset?"

Jeaneau tossed back her head and took another swig.

Lance kneeled at her side. "If the men got to him in time," he began.

"If the men got to him in time," she snorted, "then he might only suffer later from fever and malaise."

"He has a strong constitution and no ailments. Besides, I don't think the sea is ready to take him yet."

oger felt the world return, his body was no longer cold, well not all of it. What woke him was cold air brushing across his foot which had fallen out of his blanket. He pulled the foot back in and opened his eyes. His whole body hurt, and the simple act of breathing was unpleasant.

"Sir, he's awake."

"About damn time."

Roger felt the presence of someone hovering over him and opened his eyes. They were swollen and dry, so the form was blurry, but held the shape of Arthur.

"Excellent to see you alive, Edevane, but I am not pleased."

Roger attempted to sit up. "I understand Admiral. I was caught off guard."

Arthur snorted. "You were played."

Roger looked up at him. "Sir?"

"That damnable woman played you. I understand that women can make men weak, but it was your duty to watch that ship. Instead, I hear you were in her quarters behind closed doors."

"It is not what you think." He began working to get out of the bed. "She did not act in any manner unfitting…"

"It's exactly what I think. You were already soft on the woman. My fault, she already had an influence over you, but you should have never let it come between you and your duties."

He stood on shaky feet and reached for his coat. "I take full responsibility for my actions. Captain Elricksen maneuvered her ship into an escapable position, and I did not realize it. I merely assumed her ship was slower than the fleet. I should not have returned to her ship but wished to speak with her on a personal manner. She and her crew were already prepared, and I was an anomaly that she used to her advantage. At least it was I, and not my men, that had to suffer the frigid waters."

"I could suffer the loss or punishment of two marines, but what do I do with you?"

Roger stood to his full height. "I am willing to take whatever punishment you deem fit."

Arthur glared at him. "That is just it. I have no time to punish you. We have arrived at our rally point and the whole fleet is waiting for my orders to attack. I need you at your post."

Notable tension left the young captain's shoulders. "I am honored to remain under your command."

"Good. Son, I understand how a woman can affect a man's judgment, but the next time you decide to shake the sheets don't do it with an adversary."

Roger jerked at Arthur's comment and replied, "I did not and would not have taken such an action. She is also not an enemy. She was merely in the wrong place at the wrong time."

"What?" Arthur guffawed. "You did not even get a taste of the woman?"

He shook his head insulted by the insinuation. "No, sir. She is a captain of a ship and to be treated with the respect that position deserves."

"Damnable shame. She cockled you and you got nothing for it."

"Sir, I admit that Captain Elricksen bested me, but in no way did she do so in any manner unfitting a ship's captain. She caught me off guard and was able to draw her weapon on me. She then forced me to send the marines back to the ship and demanded I jump. They were the actions of a desperate captain protecting her crew."

Arthur eyed his protege. "She did not sway you into collusion?"

"No sir, there was nothing she said that persuaded my actions until she drew her sword and made her demands."

"Nothing?"

Roger stood resolute. "Nothing."

"Hunh, a waste then, if you ask me." He clapped Roger on the shoulder. "Now then, let's get to my ship and discuss tactics with the other captains. We have a King to dethrone and another one to put on it."

FOURTEEN

Land Ho!

Captain Roger Edevane stood on his ship as the sun rose on Guy Fawkes day and knew the rest of his career would change at this moment. In truth, his part in the mission was complete. He had sailed the ship from the Netherlands, filled with reserve Dutch soldiers and marines, and successfully brought them to English shores.

Avoiding interception with the English fleet, their sizeable army landed in an unprepared Torbay. As a legion of small boats escorted the soldiers to shore, his job now was to help maintain the fleet and keep the English from blocking them in. Popery would be stopped again on this auspicious day, but Roger wondered at what cost.

Throughout the day he watched the army unload and march through the small town toward England. The Prince of Orange unloaded off his skiff and step onto English soil with surety and little ceremony. Was he watching the invasion of his own country by a foreign prince for the first time in six centuries?

Even if William was a rightful heir to the English Crown, he was still a foreign prince. And despite so many failed attempts by other countries, this prince was waltzing his way to London, and nothing was going to stop him.

Lt Samuels stepped next to him and gazed over the railing. "I thought we'd see a little conflict, but we just slipped 53 ships past the English. How is that possible?"

Edevane acknowledge his second. "Quite easily when they already know we are coming and let us pass."

Samuels arched his brow.

Edevane grimaced. "This war was won before we set sail. We are merely proof that, if challenged, we will win."

"Then what do you think they will do with all this?" Samuels asked, motioning to the fleet.

Roger turned his back to England and gazed across the sea. "Popery doesn't only exist in England."

$\mathcal{J}$eaneau stepped off the bumboat and onto the dock. Standing next to a carriage in front of her was a woman covered in layers of frills and lace. The frontage on her head stood so high Jeaneau was sure it would topple in the slightest breeze. "Hello, Mother."

"Jeaneau!" she softly cried and started to reach out to embrace her daughter, but then her nose crinkled. "Heavens, you are an awful sight and smell."

"It's called being at sea." She bemoaned.

Fussingat over Jeaneau's worn hems and torn sleeves, she tisked, "And that you have been, you are a week late. Where have you been?'

Wary and in no mood to explain, she replied, "We were temporarily redirected, but I am here now."

"Good." Her mother declared and drug Jeaneau to the

carriage. "Have your first mate tend to your ship. We have things to do, but not until you clean up and look presentable."

The ride to the rented estate was filled with her mother's incessant talking about socials, salons, and gatherings of all kinds. Jeaneau stared out the window, watching the buildings and people go by.

The carriage rocked back and forth like a rough sea and she began to drift to sleep. A dream stirred in her mind. She was standing in the shallows of a rushing river full of fish. She could easily reach into the current, grab any fish she desired and hold it in her hand. However, she found no interest in any of them and would toss them back.

Above her on the shore stood Roger. He smiled at her and said, "You know where I should take you? The Rivers in Wales, the waters are so clean, and everything is green." He stepped closer. "And when the mists roll in, it's like the heaven and earth touch."

She stepped out of the water and ran her hand over his shoulder. It was strong and powerful. She kissed it through the wool coat and put her arms around him.

He reached up, stroking his fingers across her forearms.

She leaned in and whispered into his ear, "I want you."

He shuddered slightly, his mouth opened in surprise, and he replied, "But you are broken."

Jeaneau was jarred awake by the sudden stop of the carriage and inhaled sharply. She looked around in a daze, finding her mother's annoyed face looking back.

"Did you hear nothing I said?"

She sat up and smiled weakly. "I'm sorry, Mother."

Her mother started right back into her droll listing of duties and obligations arranged over the next week, but Jeaneau's thoughts drifted back to the dream, and she wondered at her own words. Why was she broken?

*J*eaneau was at a dinner party when the news of England arrived in France. The table which had been softly chatting on a myriad of mundane subjects was now ablaze with the coup.

"Damnable Protestants," one man said.

"They just can't be happy with The King God gave them."

"Never are," another diner added.

"Mlle Jeaneau, your father is Dutch. What do you think of your prince now being the King of England?"

"As long as commerce continues to move, I do not care who or who does not sit on a throne." She continued to eat her food and drink her wine.

"And if there is war?"

"War is always good for business," she replied and took another bite.

"Until someone sinks your ships."

She keenly smiled. "I do my best to avoid such things."

"But you yourself are Catholic, do you not fear persecution? Now that the Orange Prince has England, who's to say he won't finally start the war with France he has wanted so badly?"

"If the prince wants a war with France, it is with good reason."

The clinking of silverware on plates stilled around her and they all just stared.

She was not silenced by their shock. "What? It is true. Louis is constantly pushing into the lowlands. If William decides to turn his forces on France, it should be no surprise."

"Jeaneau, Darling." Her mother's voice cooed across the table. She did not utter another word, that was all she needed.

The silent message was heard loud and clear by everyone. Her mother was French to the bone. The fact that she married a foreigner just made her more French.

Jeaneau glowered at her mother.

"Do not fret, Madame Elricksen," interjected the Viscount. "I enjoy your daughter's bravado."

"Yes, but there is a time and place for such things. We are not at a coffee house."

He smiled at her mother, then drew his eyes toward Jeaneau. "Then perhaps we can discuss this further over coffee."

"Coffee, tea, or wine, I will speak my mind whenever I wish," Jeaneau replied and drank from her cup.

*J*eaneau collapsed on her bed that night, exhausted from the party. Her end table was strewn with calling cards, and she could feel her mother's match making hands tighten around her throat. She couldn't breathe.

Tearing off her clothes to get to lacings, she paced and stumbled, tossing pieces of clothing all over the room. Nearly fear of her foundations and ready to dive under the bed covers, her mother's inevitable knock rapt on the door.

"Darling," her mother called.

Jeaneau groaned. Why did she even visit her mother?

Her mother did not wait for a response and simply opened the door. "Jeaneau..." she looked around the room. "Was there an altercation in here?"

"Only with my dress." She spat, pulling out her fontange and stabbing it into the chaise.

"Darling, you really should take more care." Her mother grimaced, pinching a discarded bodice thrown over a chair.

Jeaneau plopped onto the bench of the vanity and began pulling pins from her hair.

"Wouldn't it be wiser," her mother interjected, "to simply wrap your hair for the night, rather than make Monique put it up again in the morning?"

"It's heavy," Jeaneau retorted.

"Most women have to add to their hair to get it that high."

Jeaneau rolled her eyes. "More hair on my head? No thank you." She picked up shears from the table. "Let's do less. Maybe I will shave my head." Glancing at the mirror, she saw her mother behind her freeze in horror. "Yes, I think shaving my head would be an excellent notion. Much better for sea travel. Less to bother with. Plus, no chance of lice."

Jeaneau's words were precise. She knew her mother both envied and cherished her hair. When she was young, Jeaneau would allow the ship's barber to shave her head when lice became an issue on board. She enjoyed the freedom it gave her. No braiding, primping, brushing, or securing.

She knew many women had thin hair and refused to be seen in public unless they had elaborate pompadours on their head. Jeaneau's hair was thick and unique in color making it easy to create the mound of curls that was desirable. She also loved her hair and was quite vain about it, so despite threatening to cut her hair, it was simply to get a reaction out of her mother. The comment worked. Her mother's face contort in disapproval and suspicion that she was being teased.

Her mother picked up the comb and began to run it through Jeaneau's hair. "About this evening. You should temper your words."

Jeaneau scoffed.

"If war is imminent, it is better to not incur the wrath of the government by making seditious comments about the monarch."

"He's not my monarch."

Her hand tightened, pulling Jeaneau's hair. "He is mine, making him yours when you are here."

"No, Mother, just yours. I wasn't born French."

"Well then, when you are married."

"Only if I marry a Frenchman."

"That has been arranged."

Jeaneau stiffened. "What?"

"Jeaneau you are nearly five and twenty."

"I am five and twenty," she replied, mocking her mother's tone.

"And I have received numerous offers. There is one we simply can't refuse."

"I can refuse."

"A contract has been made."

"Father would never sign such a document."

"I am certain he won't refuse."

Jeaneau thrust herself up from the bench and whirled on her mother. "I am not a commodity mother. I cannot be bought and sold like chattel."

"All women are commodities, Darling. Anyone can be bought and sold for a price."

"Not you! You were not contracted to my father. You chose to run off to sea with him."

"Yes, and where has that left me? I could be a nobleman's wife rather than the wife of a sea merchant."

Jeaneau hated the disgust in her mother's voice. That was her father. Just because her mother regretted her past decisions did not give her the right to decide hers. She grimaced. "An arranged marriage? It's barbaric."

"You buy and sell items all the time. How is this any different?"

"Because I don't sell myself, and if I did, it would be by my choice, not yours."

"Then choose. The company is nearly finished. We are

losing contracts every day, and both you and your father refuse to join the VOC. Who, by the way, did not look favorably on your last refusal and have banned us from more ports. Fewer ports, fewer places to ship, means less contacts and less money. If we do not ally with someone soon, we will fail."

She slumped down into a chair. "So you will sell me."

"A marriage need not be slavery, Darling."

"I know very few men who don't consider a wife property and human property is slavery, mother."

"But you can marry well. Fine clothes, delicious food."

"Being told where to sit and what to say." She lamented.

"Why do you have such an intolerable view on marriage? Your father and I do love each other."

"Precisely. You chose to marry. I am being given no choice."

"You wish for a choice? Fine, you have a table full of choices." She motioned to the pile of calling cards.

"And why can't I choose not to marry?"

"You can choose to do so," her mother flatly replied. "And the company will fail."

"Is there not another solution? Would you be so insistent if I was Claude?"

"If there was a woman he could marry that would bring in the same wealth, then yes I would. But your brother isn't here, and he's abandoned the family. Will you do the same?"

Jeaneau frowned. Her heart ached with anger, guilt, and shame. The day she dreaded was now upon her. "Must he be French?"

"He could be English for all I care, as long as he has the money to invest and will agree to only invest and let your father run the company."

"And after father dies, do you think such a man would still let me run the company?"

Her mother's jaw dropped. "You?"

"It is my legacy, Mother."

"It is your father's legacy. You are the daughter, not the son."

"Claude is a criminal and a thief who left us, but has more rights to the company than me? I have always been here making sure the company doesn't fail. I know the business as well as my father and can run it."

"But your place is to be a wife, not run a business."

"Women run businesses all the time. Why should I not be allowed such liberties?"

"Because you are not a washerwoman. You are the daughter of a rich merchant who can be more."

"If more means sitting around all day barking at servants and doing needlework, I'd much rather wash clothes. Besides, even England had a queen."

"Who died a virgin."

"Oh, please Mother. Not married maybe, but virgin?"

Her mother rubbed her face in frustration. "Jeaneau, why must you be so difficult?"

"Because my mother wishes to sell me to the highest bidder, so I can lay around all day and get fat."

"Peasants dream of a life that would make them fat. But you!" Her mother pointed a finger at her. "You want to live off bare essentials and brown under the heat of the sun."

"If I could tan I would do it happily, and there is nothing wrong with rationing food."

"Manual labor, closed quarters, the stench of men…these are the things my daughter enjoys!" She declared, throwing her hands in the air.

Jeaneau dropped her head into her hands and massaged her temple. "No, Mother. Fresh air, boundless seas, and freedom from the rules of men. That's what I enjoy." She lifted her head. "Meeting new people, seeing new lands. Realizing that the world goes far beyond these shores. Our society is not the only one, nor the right one. They say that in the Americas, women choose who they can marry, and they can also divorce. And when she decides to make the man leave, she keeps everything. Can you imagine?"

Her mother threw the comb on the table. "You are wanting to live like a savage? My child has gone mad!"

Jeaneau ran her fingers through her hair. "I'm not mad, mother. I just want to be treated less like property and more like…like a man."

She scoffed. "If you think men are free then you know nothing. Every man is owned by someone. His boss, his lord, his god. No man is free, and all have obligations." She wagged a finger at her daughter. "And before you say men don't have to marry, believe me, they do. Our society is built on marriage contracts. Your own prince married that English princess because of obligation, but he made the best of it and now will become King of England. So, you can concede to the fact that marriage is crucial to survival and be involved in the process or be forced into it. Either way, it will happen, so I suggest you choose the less painful route."

Jeaneau's skin dulled, she looked away from her mother and stared at a random point on the wall. If she chose something to stare at, to focus on perhaps, she could stop the screaming in her head. "Very well, Mother."

"What?"

"I said very well, but I will be part of the process."

Her mother practically applauded as she filled with glee. "Excellent. I will gather my list and we will discuss it over breakfast. If I am lucky, we will have you engaged by the yuletide and married in the spring."

Jeaneau drew her feet up into the chair and under her chemise. Her arms wrapped around her knees and her eyes never left the spot as she gently nodded in agreement.

Her mother rushed over and kissed her on the top of the head and practically danced out the door.

Jeaneau stared at the spot, as her heart slowly died. She could sense her freedom slipping away and heavy weights dragging at her body. Overwhelming dread began to consume her. The dread of martial obligation. The fear of being told to stay at home and not go to sea. No man she had ever met, no man that ever pursued her even, thought she would keep sailing, not even Rafe.

Burying her head into her knees, she worked every possible option, every angle, and all left her hopeless. She came to one viable conclusion but knew it would have its own repercussions.

Lifting her head, she listened to the house. Nearly all movement had ceased. No servants stirred, and her mother very likely took a draught to help her sleep soundly.

Once she was sure no one was awake, she quietly slipped out of the chair and crept out of her room. She carefully walked down the hallway and into the room adjacent to her mother's room. Hurrying towards a large chest, she unlatched it and hoped that the hinges would not squeak too loudly.

As they moaned and creaked, she paused to make sure her mother didn't stir. Once the lid was open, she deftly removed the desired items. Out came trousers, a shirt, coat, and boots. She looked around the room to see if she could find a hat.

In a box, never worn, sat a brand new broad brimmed hat. It was a brilliant blue with way too many plumes. Clearly a gift for her father, but Jeaneau thought it would go well with her own blue coat. She put the hat on her head, gathered up the clothes and slunk back to her room. There she quickly, but cautiously, grabbed the few items she would not leave behind and put on her father's clothes.

Thankfully her father was not much taller than her and men's clothes always had ample room, so they did not look too loose on her slightly smaller frame. She let her hair fall loose at her sides, which was always her preference. Putting the hat on her head, she picked up her bag and boots and departed her mother's abode for the last time.

Her heart raced as she moved through the streets and

towards the docks. Very few people paid her notice, assuming she was just another man walking. Each step shed her feeling of dread till she found herself at the dock.

Nearby, a bumboat rocked in the water, with its owner sound asleep. She kicked the boat. The owner jolted awake, causing his boat to rock back and forth. She helped steady the boat with her foot. "I need to board the Daughter's Fortune."

"Now?"

"Yes, now."

"It will cost you double."

"I will pay one and a half."

The man softly grumbled.

"And I will help row."

The man straightened and grabbed the oars. "Fair 'nuff."

Jeaneau stepped in and took the oars. Every stroke and every exhale was exhilarating. She could feel freedom draw closer. By the time she arrived at the ship her muscles ached, but she glowed with satisfaction.

A crewman of Daughter's Fortune looked down to the unscheduled arrival, concerned. "Is there something amiss? Why are you here?"

"It is your captain," Jeaneau called back. "Lower the rope."

Jean-Pierre heard the commotion and arrived in time to see a hat full of feathers cap the railing.

He looked to the sailor who replied, "It's the captain, but she's…"

Jean-Pierre reached out and helped her land on the deck and then looked at her quite baffled. There she stood in front of him wearing men's clothes and the biggest smile on her face. "My God, you look like your brother!"

"Do I?" she replied and looked at herself. "The hat is a bit much, but the trousers fit."

"Jeaneau, what are you doing here?"

"Oh!" she said happily. "Call me Auvilda!" she replied.

"Oh no."

"Mother, she wants me to marry."

"Yes…"

"Well, I thought about it and the only way she could actually get me married is if she sees me, so…we are leaving."

"Leaving?"

"Yes, leaving. If I am not here, she can't force me to marry."

"I'm not quite following, Jeaneau."

"Simple. The only men she would choose for me to marry are not going to marry someone who refuses to stop living at sea. I know no man that she would want for me that would be willing to be a captain's…wife, so if I don't come to shore, she can't get me married."

"You are going to stay at sea…indefinitely."

"Oh, I am sure I can go to shore in places she isn't at, but as far as a home. This is now my home, no other."

"And your father?"

"I'm not worried about my father, but if my mother claims that I need a husband to make sure this company stays afloat, let's prove her wrong." She pulled a bundle out of her bag and handed it to him. He unraveled it and found gold trinkets. "We will sell this and go see Gustave."

"Gustave?"

"Yes. It's about time we did. The ship needs a few improvements."

"Improvements for what exactly?"

"England has a new king, and that king has no love for France. And France has no love for either England or their new king. War is imminent."

"We are not a warship."

"No, but both sides will be needing ships to transport goods, supplies, and secrets."

"Jeaneau, you detest such matters."

"I do, but I detest being forced into marriage even more."

Jean-Pierre was baffled at her statement but could see the zeal in her eyes. "I will have what crew is on shore collected and we will sail at the tide."

She leaned over and kissed him on the cheek.

He exhaled deeply dreading the impending danger, but then gave her a soft smirk. "Careful," he replied, forcing a mirthful tone, "dressed like that I might get aroused."

FIFTEEN

Changing Course

Jeaneau felt her body slowly begin to wake. She shifted slightly and grinned softly at the feel of the soft down blanket covering her. She dug deeper into its warmth trying to ignore the chill in the air. A hand touched her, pulling back her hair, and she felt lips kiss the back of her neck. Rolling over, she found Gustave on the edge of her bed, grinning back.

"Sleep well?" he asked.

She wriggled under the layers of warmth. "Very much so. And you?"

"Alas, I did not sleep as soundly. I missed…companionship."

"You mean you missed me in your bed."

"Yes," he replied kindly and leaned down for a kiss.

She slipped an arm free from her covers and placed her finger on his lips. "I said this just needed to be business."

He groaned softly. "And why no pleasure with our business?"

She sat up against the headboard. "Do you get into bed with your other business partners?"

Gustave shrugged. "As opportunity arises." He picked up

her hand and kissed it tenderly. His eyes lifted and locked with hers.

She adored his eyes and dark brows. "You are incorrigible."

"I agree." He leaned in, kissing her neck again.

She felt herself give under his touch. "How is my ship?" she asked, trying to keep her mind clear, but her fingers slipped into his hair.

He slid his hand under the covers and across her legs. "Her flanks are strong."

She gasped lightly and grasped the back of his neck.

His hand moved deeper into the blanket and cupped her rear. "But her underside needs attention."

Jeaneau's thoughts clashed violently in her head. She could not understand why she hesitated in being with Gustave. She never had before. Each time she came in for repairs, she allowed herself time to not be a captain, to not worry about duties and obligations.

He treated her like a goddess, and she loved the attention. As her mind fought internally, pleasure was winning, and she was unclothing him. He knew where and when to touch her.

She inhaled sharply. "The ship," she said, trying to gain control.

"Is being tended to, now to tend to you," Gustave replied as he coaxed more pleasure from her lips.

"I need tending?" she gasped.

"Oh yes, let me see to your needs."

There was pleasure in letting go and her body relented to his touch. Part of her tried to argue that she wanted to be better, but the argument got lost in the warmth and ecstasy.

*T*hey laid there breathing heavy and in utter bliss.

Her fingers trailed across his sweaty body. "This has to stop."

"Why?"

"I'm trying to be better?"

"Better at what? My dear, you are already quite remarkable."

"I am more than something to be bedded."

"I quite agree."

"Then why do I find it is bedding a man, or at least making them think as such, is the only way to get what I need?"

He turned and looked at her. "Jeaneau, do you think I would not work on your ships if you did not come to my bed?"

She remained silent and looked away.

He chuckled softly. "My dear, your charms are quite formidable. I assume you use them the way you do, because of their power."

"I do," she admitted with some disgust.

"But you are not merely flesh, Jeaneau. There is something about you that goes beyond your beguiling looks. Something most men would tremble at if they understood it fully."

She looked back at him, curious.

"You live in a world of men, and you do not cower." He leaned onto his side and propped his head up on his hand. "Most men at this moment would assume they had overpowered you, that you relented because they are a man, and you are a woman. I know that if you truly had not wished for me to be in your bed, you would have fought and defeated me."

"Would you have taken me, if I had fought?"

"You? No."

"Others?"

"I have never been in such a situation. Granted there were times last night I thought of bursting into this room."

"But you didn't."

"No, passion is one thing, but good business is more important."

"Or the fact that, since I have laid with you before, you knew I would eventually give in."

His lips pursed impishly. "Well, there is that."

"And what if next time I say no?"

His brow furrowed. "Why would you?"

"If I was married."

He burst out laughing.

"Or in love with another."

"Ah…see the first is hard to believe, but love…Can Jeaneau allow herself to love?"

"You question if I can love, but still lie with me."

"Sex is entirely separate from love."

"That's what I said!" she declared.

"You said? To whom?"

"Oh…this captain. We were discussing the politics of marriage."

"Really? What man has the power to make Jeaneau question her motives?"

"No one," she replied and shifted her night dress back over her body. "If I change my mind, it is on my own terms."

"Of course. Does this mean you wish to renegotiate the terms of our relationship?"

"That attempt apparently failed."

He chuckled. "My apologies. If you wish to change our terms, I am willing to enter into discussion."

She eyed him. "I am sure you will."

"Come," he said, slapping her thigh. "I came to fetch you for breakfast. I am sure my cooks will be fretting, trying to keep it warm and fresh."

She sat at his table and enjoyed the fresh food, though he was right, most of it was slightly overdone. Nevertheless, she devoured the fresh fruit, sipped the tea, and enjoyed the fresh butter on her bread.

Gustave watched her eat, a smile cross his face. "How is your cook on the ship?"

Jeaneau snorted. "My cook is great, but also the surgeon. The biggest issue will be getting fresh supplies. Especially with the war coming."

"You are so sure it is coming."

"Oh yes."

"It is a good thing we installed those faux gun ports."

"It's a good thing I suggested the working shutters."

"Have you used them?"

She looked at him and grinned with glee. "Yes, nearly got us shot!"

"I thought the point was to keep you from getting attacked."

"Yes, and I am sure they have helped, but when you come across a fleet…" She stopped herself from saying more.

"A fleet." His eyes darted in realization. "You saw the fleet from Amsterdam!"

She stopped mid-bite, trying to answer this correctly. "I… may have come across a series of ships sailing from that direction…"

"Jeaneau, how are you here? How did you escape?"

"Who says I was caught?"

He examined her face. "If someone did come across a military fleet on its way to commit a coup, I am sure they would be very lucky to escape un…affected."

"Very lucky," she said, holding his gaze a moment longer then went back to eating.

"You are a remarkable woman, Jeaneau."

"I'm a remarkable sea captain."

He raised his teacup to her. "That you are."

A servant stepped in with the morning post and Gustave perused it. He examined one letter and opened it.

Jeaneau took little notice as she continued to eat.

He glanced over and asked, "Were you not supposed to be taking this winter in France with your mother?"

She stopped chewing and looked at him for a long moment. Putting her fork down, she replied, "I was."

"I knew your ship was coming, but I only expected Jean-Pierre."

"I decided I'd rather see you than waste my time in France."

"Yes, because my secluded port is more interesting."

"Perhaps I was seeking peace and quiet?" she said through a full mouth.

He fanned the letter lightly. "Or avoiding your mother."

"I'd find any excuse to ignore her," she said bluntly. "Is that from her?"

"Yes, she has written to know if I have seen you."

Jeaneau snorted. "Quite a bit of me."

He chuckled again. "She says you are to be married soon, and if I see you, to send word."

Jeaneau threw her napkin onto her plate, thrust herself up from the table, and began pacing back and forth in front of the long set of windows.

"Is this what you spoke of earlier?" Gustave asked, "Are you getting married?"

"Not if I can help it."

He carefully set down the letter, rose from his chair, and walked over to her. She was boiling with anger and frustration.

It was terrifying and beautiful. He gently placed his hands on her shoulders. "Explain."

"What is there to explain? My mother thinks it would be better for me and the company if I marry. In her mind, I am merely a tool to wealth."

"Or she wants to ensure you have a stable future."

"I can have a stable future without a husband."

"As a sea captain?"

"Yes."

"A sea captain's life is often short and full of failure."

"You agree with her." Her eyes blazed. "I should come to shore and slowly die of boredom?"

His mouth twitched in a half smile. "Is living on land such a deplorable notion?"

"Living on land, trapped in a loveless marriage. Yes, that sounds rather deplorable."

"What if it wasn't loveless?"

"I would still be trapped on land."

"What if he permitted you to still sail?"

She laughed out loud. "And what if unicorns were real." She continued to giggle until her eyes met his.

He held her at arm's length so she could clearly see his face.

"Gustave,"

"I think I would meet your mother's approval for wealth and security. We could even set up a storehouse next to the shipyard. I am sure another point of export would please her."

She was stunned. The rush of emotions, options, opportunities, and outcomes was so overwhelming that she just stood there.

He stroked her face. "Jeaneau, I adore you. I don't expect you to love me, but you do like me. We work well together and enjoy each other's company. If marrying me stops your mother's incessant meddling and if I promise to let you keep sailing?"

"You would do that." She studied his face. "You would let me keep sailing."

He ran his fingers through her hair. "Yes, just make me your first port of call."

Captain Roger Edevane rubbed his hands together, willing warmth into them. His face peeked out from the scarf thickly wrapped around his neck and face. He glanced at Lt. Samuels who was also tucked tightly in his own garments, hiding from the chilly air.

Roger shifted his feet and checked his pocket watch. "Our shift is nearly over. Ready to go below and eat something warm?"

Samuels looked back at him. "Then I shouldn't tell you I see a very suspicious ship."

Roger looked over the Lt.'s shoulder and across the gray water. Far from the shore and heading their direction was a single-masted skiff. It sat heavy and bobbed across the rough water. "Fisherman with a heavy haul?"

"Sailing away from the shore after dusk?"

"Out for a sail?"

"In this weather?" retorted Samuels

"We're out here."

"Not by choice."

Roger sighed and lifted his glass to get a closer look. A sailor aboard lifted a covered lantern and passed his hand over it allowing light to flash three times. "He's signaling for assistance. Change course."

"Aye, Captain," Samuels replied and sent the order to move towards the skiff.

As they approached, they could see it was laden with more men than required for a boat its size. Many of the men huddled to the center of the craft.

Roger called out, "Ahoy."

"Ahoy," a man called back.

"Is everything well? We noticed you are heading away from shore?"

"We were out fishing and came across a very fine catch. We noticed that we were far out and then saw your ship," the man replied in an excited tone. "Seeing your colors and armament we thought you might like what we caught."

Roger leaned over the railing into the ship below. "And what did you catch? Carp?"

The man speaking turned and looked over his shoulder. "It ain't carp, more like a kingfish."

Roger looked to his Lt with a quizzical expression and then back to the skiff.

Amongst the huddled mass in the center, one man stood up and said, "I should have known better. After all, you are my Navy."

Roger looked at the man and felt a knot form in his throat. He had never met him, but knew his countenance. It was King James. Conflict thrashed inside of him, but he hid his surprise. "Then you know I am also bound to bring you in, Your Majesty."

The king nodded.

SIXTEEN

Prize Law

"Gustave?"

"Yes, Gustave."

"But–" Jean-Pierre took off his glasses and pinched his nose. "Didn't we just flee your mother's house because she wanted you to marry?"

"She wanted me to marry some ancient braggart of her choosing. That would whirl me about on his arm for status."

"Gustave is not young."

"He's not old either and I…we have known him for a long time."

"Yes, we have," he replied grimly.

"Good Lord, Jean-Pierre. It is a good offer. He will let me keep sailing and he's offered to build an additional storehouse. If that isn't a desirable offer, then I'm not sure what is."

"So, he gets your future holdings and is willing to let you sail out to sea, increasing your chance of dying and leaving him everything."

"If he dies, I will get his holdings. He has no heirs."

"If he chooses to do so. And until you give him an heir."

"Ha! I can avoid that."

He frowned. "He's a rake."

"If you are insinuating that he has been with other women—"

"—and men."

"You're one to talk!" she huffed. "Besides, I would like to remind you that I am well known for my libertine ways."

"And will the two of you continue in such…activities?"

"What does that matter?"

"Perhaps not for him so much, but if you do get pregnant."

"Jean-Pierre!"

"A man does not take it lightly when a woman is pregnant with another man's child."

"But if he continues in such a manner, I am to accept it?"

"That is up to you, but what if he does have a bastard. How would you feel?"

She pinched her brow. "Do I really have a better offer?"

"You could continue to not marry?"

"And then my mother would devise a contract binding me to an intolerable marriage and my only choices would be to marry or break completely free from my family, our company."

"Do you love him?"

"Good God." She tossed her hands in the air, and continued to pace. "What does love have to do with marriage?"

"You planned to marry Louie for love."

She glared at him. "And look where that got me!"

"You can't blame the sea."

"I most certainly can!" She growled and fell into a chair. Despite the skirts, she sat in the seat, legs spread apart, and propped her foot on a second chair. "It's a good offer."

Jean-Pierre crouched next to her. "Will he make you happy?"

"I will be far from unhappy. He understands me and is insanely good in bed."

"That is certainly a bonus."

She laughed softly and sniffled. Jean-Pierre always got to the heart of her.

"I can speak with him. Make sure he treats you fairly."

She peered at him through her fingers and gave him a loving grin. "I can negotiate my own terms."

"Then consider me your second."

There was a knock at the drawing room door and Gustave sheepishly appeared. "The yelling stopped."

"We do that," Jeaneau said as she stood up. "He would not be a good first mate if he didn't make sure I was certain in my actions."

"Are you?" Gustave asked.

"I am."

He beamed.

"But a contract will still need to be made and I'd like to have formalities concluded as quickly as possible," Jeaneau insisted.

"Then I should call my solicitor?"

"And your priest," Jean-Pierre added.

He took grand steps toward her and excitedly embraced her hands in his. "I shall endeavor to make you happy."

Jean-Pierre stepped closer to Jeaneau. "And I shall keep you to that promise."

*A*rthur bellowed, "You arrested him?"

Roger looked baffled. "As we were ordered."

Arthur threw his hands in the air. "When will you learn to read through orders?"

"Sir?"

"Congratulations. You have captured the dethroned king,

now the new king will have to either behead him or some other spectacle, and that will only make the man a martyr." He poured himself a glass of brandy. "This was to be a bloodless coup. If he kills The King there will be discontent and a lot more blood."

"What were we supposed to do? The fishermen that caught him would have talked."

"Not if they didn't make it back to shore," Arthur mumbled into his glass.

"They were doing their duty to the new king."

"Yes, yes," Arthur replied flippantly. "But now we have two kings and one crown. If William kills him, the unrest will last longer than desired."

Roger pondered for a moment. "What if James were to escape again?"

"Then William will look the fool. The baby is already in France. To allow James to escape would make the military look weak."

"Can't the King simply let him go?"

Arthur stopped mid-sip. "Or in goodwill allow him to leave." He slowly drew in another sip. "As a tempered ruler would. One of tolcrance and forgiveness."

Roger knew that look well. Arthur was devising a plan, and while brilliant, those in its wake could suffer.

SEVENTEEN

Head to the Wind

*J*eaneau was chewing on toast and jam when the door to the breakfast room opened.

Gustave looked up from the correspondence he was reading and took the new message from the servant. "Special Courier," the servant said. "He waits for a reply."

"Who's it from?" she asked.

"I do not know," Gustave said. "It's addressed to you."

"Me? Who knows I am here?"

"Many. Now," he replied and smiled.

She picked up her knife smeared in butter and opened the letter. Inside was another letter with a royal seal. "Good God," she muttered in shock. "Is this?" She showed it to Gustave, "Is this his seal?"

Gustave tried to discern the seal, but before he could, she broke it and read the letter.

She quickly paled and then looked at him. "I'm being summoned by the prince!"

"Our prince?"

"Yes, our prince. Also the future King of England. He is summoning me and the Daughter's Fortune to go to London."

"Why…" He looked completely baffled.

Jeaneau looked annoyed. "That damnable Old Man Smith. I know he is behind this. Jean-Pierre told me you get in bed with an Englishman and they expect you to do anything else they want."

She pushed herself away from the table and began to pace.

Gustave wondered if this sight would be a regular appearance in his breakfast room.

She paced back and forth, alternating from staring at the letter to then thrusting it away from her eyes and pacing some more.

The servant cleared his throat. "The courier."

"The courier. I'll tell the courier what I think!" Still wearing her night dress, untethered dressing gown, and her hair flowing free, she burst out the door and towards the entryway.

"Jeaneau!" Gustave cried and rushed after her. "What are you going to tell the courier? It is a summons from our prince."

"Prince or no prince," she bellowed, "I am no pawn." She saw the figure standing in the hall and shouted, "You!"

The figure heard her entrance and was already turning.

Jeaneau slammed to a halt and her jaw dropped. "Roger!"

Roger, in unsurmountable decorum, bowed to the half-dressed, and furious Jeaneau. "Captain Elricksen."

"What are you…Why…That damnable Smith."

"Yes, Lord Admiral Torrington thought it best to send me."

"What is this about? Is he still after my ship? Is he using this alliance for his own petty revenge because I bested him? Why does he have the Prince summoning me?"

"From my understanding, The King is requesting your assistance."

"Doesn't he now have two fleets under his reign? What can I possibly do?"

Gustave cleared his throat. "Jeaneau, perhaps we can discuss this sitting down."

Roger looked at Gustave and bowed again. "I assume you are the Master of this House. I apologize for my intrusion. Captain Roger Edevane of the British Navy."

Gustave shook the man's hand, but could not hide his confusion. "This is all very odd. I thought she was summoned by the Orange Prince."

"She was," Roger confirmed. "But he is presently in London securing his crown and he needs Jeaneau's help."

"I think I've done enough," Jeaneau snapped.

Gustave looked between the two. "What have you done, Jeaneau?"

Roger shifted slightly. "Perhaps we should discuss this in private. No need to endanger Mr. Oostwal."

"Captain Elricksen and I are married," Gustave interjected. "Clearly, I need to be informed and ensure my bride is protected."

Jeaneau's head slowly turned toward Gustave and she spat the word, "Protected?"

"I am merely suggesting that your concerns are my concerns and I wish to endeavor to help if I can."

Her anger continued to boil, as she walked away from them both and into the sitting room. She plopped down into a chair and waited for them to enter.

The two men came in and sat down. Roger was across from her and Gustave to her side.

"Captain Elricksen, before I begin, do you wish to explain?" Roger's eyes shifted to Gustave.

"I do not!" she snapped. "You just get to the point."

"I cannot explain to you why you are summoned, but that it is of the utmost urgency and will ensure that this coup remains relatively bloodless."

"He all but has his crown. What does he need me and my ship for?"

"He is requesting that you transport an item of importance from England to France."

"And once again it can't go on one of his many ships."

"It cannot. You have free travel between Dutch, English, and French ports."

"So do other ships."

"We do not know other ships and their captains. The Lord Admiral argued that you are the best choice because you have the necessary neutrality, the skills to sail deftly if under pursuit, and the loyalty of a crew that will keep silent."

"High praise," Gustave uttered. "This Torrington knows you well."

She leaned forward. "What am I transporting?"

"I am not at liberty to say."

She crossed her legs and leaned back. "Then I am not at liberty to do it."

Roger exhaled hard. "You will be compensated."

She scoffed.

"He is correct. Your prince now has the purse strings of two kingdoms," Gustave added.

She rolled her eyes and crossed her arms. "Untaxed port access and exclusion from ever being a bounty ship."

Roger nodded, but then said, "I am sure you can negotiate your compensation, but you will have to do that with him. You need to go to England, and quickly."

"My ship. It's dry-docked for repairs."

"Actually," Gustave intervened, "we were putting it to water this morning." He looked at Jeaneau and grinned. "Surprise…"

"My crew, they are set up for the winter. I only have half close by."

"A small crew might be the best option."

"I am sure we can supplement if necessary," Gustave added.

"It's December! I know it is just the channel, but…"

"Here to London then London to France. I have been patrolling these waters the past months and the winter has been mild."

"This is madness!"

"It is a request from your sovereign," Roger pushed.

"He is in power because he is the stadholder, not the prince."

"Either way."

She huffed, flinging herself into the back of the chair and draping her arms across the shoulders. Scowling at him, she asked, "How did you even find me?"

"We let you go, but the Lord Admiral had to be sure you wouldn't talk. You did land in France after our encounter."

"To see my mother."

He nodded. "You were being watched when you uprooted in the middle of the night and came here. He had to be sure you were not trading secrets."

She sat up a little and bared her hands. "What secrets do I have to share? Your coup was successful."

Roger shifted slightly at the word, coup. "But we had to be sure."

"Your secrets are safe with me."

"As we have seen and therefore that is why the Lord Admiral has requested you for this mission."

"Does he keep forgetting I'm not English?"

"But you are Dutch and still under your Stadtholder's command."

She rubbed her face. "Perhaps I should have married a Frenchman. Doubt he'd ask for me then."

"Jeaneau, this is an honor," Gustave encouraged.

"No, this is forced subjugation! Something I tend to avoid." She glowered at Roger. "Haplessly helping your Lord Admiral has been nothing but trouble. If I agree, I risk my ship and crew. Yet if I refuse, I am sure the punishment will be worse."

"Then you do agree."

She tossed a hand in the air. "I see no other choice."

He stood and bowed. "I came to shore by longboat, so I would not be slowed by the tide. I will have to return with your message. I need you to follow as quickly as possible."

"No escort?" she asked with a slight mock in her tone.

"No, you understand why?"

"Yes, yes. I'm sure I can find some reason to dock in English waters."

Gustave's voice gently cut into the conversation. "Perhaps, shopping for a future event? Some English Lace to take to a French Draper?"

"Are you encouraging this?"

"Well," he said, "having done a favor for a Dutch Prince and English King might be helpful to future business."

*J*eaneau couldn't believe it. She was standing in a hall waiting to speak to a king's advisor. Less than six months ago, she had to sit in a galley and wait to be permitted to even enter the court of a port authority. Now she was going to be escorted to the king himself. She felt tiny in the grand hallway and tried to slow her pounding heart.

She brushed the wrinkles smooth from her dress, allowing her fingers to run over the embroidered orange and blue flowers. Her frontage started to slip, and she adjusted it. How women wore these daily baffled her. She longed to be in her scarves and coat.

Wringing her hands, she lightly paced, wondering what favor he would ask and more importantly what she should ask in return. Any advantage would help. It would be imbecilic to think because the king requested her presence that she had the upper hand, but tilting into the wind might be the best tactic.

She thought about the voyage ahead of her. Roger was correct, the waters were favorable, but she did not know for how long. After her rush to get here, they now made her wait. "Ah!" she exhaled in frustration.

The massive door creaked open.

Jumping at the sound, she let out a sigh of relief noticing it was Roger. "Captain," she said in a warm but civil tone.

"Captain Elricksen, they are ready." He motioned for her to join him.

They walked down another long hall that seemed to swallow all light.

Roger spoke, "I see you chose your orange and blue dress. I rather expected your sailing attire."

"To see the King?" she asked, astonished.

He nodded.

"I appreciate that he is willing to allow a female Captain with this…mission, but out of respect I will dress in my best."

"Perhaps we should get you a new coat then?"

"Oh." She laughed. "Maybe in red with some gold trim. I have one in my chest presently."

"I would like to get that back."

"Maybe I will keep it. If I am to be pressed into service, I will have a nice men's coat to wear. I could let my hair down and blend right in."

He chuckled, "I don't think even the Lord Admiral is so bold as to have a known female officer in his ranks."

She smiled. "Who says I would be known? It's rather easy to dress as a man."

"And dangerous if caught."

"If," she smiled again. "Besides, I think you look better in this blue." She studied the color and examined the silver trim. "Quite nice. The red was too bold."

"You do not think me bold?"

"Well…" She stopped, pondering the question. "While you did jump off my ship, overall, you are quite reserved."

"I am tactical," he responded.

"Was that the choice you made when you helped with this…revolution?"

"I, like you, was caught unaware."

"Oh?"

He softly nodded. "The Lord Admiral only reveals information as needed. Likely his years in parliament. I, as his subordinate, must comply. Most of the time it works out."

"Happy to use others at his whim."

"Men of power do as they wish."

She paused and looked at him. "I hope when you reach such a rank, you don't."

"I am moved by your faith in my advancement." He touched his chest, bowed, and replied, "For you, I will endeavor not to be callously ambitious."

She smiled and proceeded forward.

"I have not wished you well on your marriage."

She tried not to tense but ended up grasping her hands and chuckling lightly. "A business arrangement."

"You did say marriage is but a contract."

And sex an addendum, she thought in her head. Tossing her head back, she brandished a smile, though it did not show the same sincerity as the one she just gave. "It was either Gustave or some other less tolerable choice."

"So, he is…tolerable?"

She looked at him, exposing more of herself than usual. "Tolerable enough."

They had reached the door.

He turned, facing her fully, and said, "Then I wish you nothing but happiness for your future."

"Thank you." Her mind raced to change the subject. "And I am glad you are not dead."

"Dead?"

"I did drop you into the Channel."

"You did what a captain must to protect her crew."

She smiled again. She liked that he never seemed to doubt her position as a captain. "Despite my dedication to their future, I am glad to see that I did not rob you of yours." On impulse, she reached out and took his hand to emphasize her meaning.

Her reaction to touching him shocked her. She realized that in every previous encounter, they had never once actually touched. There was still a glove between his flesh and hers, but the connection was apparent.

His hand moved, but instead of pulling away, it rolled over hers to return the gentle grasp. His thumb ran over her mount of Venus, and she shivered.

They simultaneously pulled away and looked at each other in silence. Before either could speak the door opened.

One of The King's secretaries stepped out and guided them in.

Sitting behind a large table stacked with maps, letters, books, and missives was William Prince of Orange. Standing, near a window, was Lord Admiral Torrington, aka Arthur Herbert.

Arthur turned and beamed at their arrival. "Excellent. I was starting to wonder if you two had gotten…delayed on your way in. Is that a flush in your cheeks, Captain Elricksen?"

William scratched his nose lightly as he assessed her response.

Jeaneau's eyes narrowed in anger but she attempted to remain calm. She did not look at Captain Edevane, refusing to give Arthur any further ammunition.

William gauged that she was a woman of good stock. Merchant class most assuredly, but not what he expected from a sea captain. He admired her gown and attempted composure, despite Arthur's comments.

He shuffled a few papers then spoke. "Captain Elricksen, I am told you have agreed to assist me in a mission of utmost importance."

"Yes, Stadtholder."

His brow arched at the title she chose to use and found it satisfactory. In one word she identified his position in her eyes. She was Dutch and was making that clear. In kind he continued the rest of his questions in Dutch.

"Your ship is sound?"

"Newly refitted."

"And you can travel to French ports safely."

"I can."

"Do you have issues with your passenger?"

"It is a passenger and not a message?"

"It is."

"Who?"

"The former sovereign of this country."

Jeaneau paled. "The King of England."

"Yes, the former King of England. Do you have issues with this?"

"No," she said slowly, still grasping the ramifications of the request. "He is not my sovereign."

A door in the back of the room cracked open and Mary glided in. "William?" she began then stopped, seeing strangers. Her relaxed composure changed as she approached and examined the two new arrivals.

"Mary," William said, "this is the captain who will be sailing the ship to take your father to his new residence."

Mary nodded to Captain Edevane. "Thank you for this service to your country." She then looked at William. "I thought we were sending him with a merchant captain?"

"We are," William replied. "Meet Captain Jeaneau Elricksen."

Jeaneau dropped her head and curtsied.

"A woman?"

"Yes, and according to the Lord Admiral, a fine and trustworthy captain."

William watched Mary study her. He knew she was questioning the use of a woman for the mission to take her father to France. Despite the repercussions, she wanted to make certain her father lived, as any daughter would.

"With England's history of strong leading women," William said, "I thought you would approve."

"Is she capable?"

"Indeed she is, Your Highness," Arthur said between gulps. "Captain Elricksen has been essential in securing your husband's future in England and not once has she or her crew told another of her role."

"Are you married, Captain?" Mary asked.

"I am."

"And your husband permits you to sail."

"Yes," she spoke.

William saw the slightest twitch in the Lady Captain's jaw.

"And your husband sails with you?" Mary inquired.

"No."

"And he is accepting of this."

She politely smiled. "He is."

William liked her. Solid, stoic, assured. If her ship was anything like her, it was formidable. He wondered why Mary was interrogating her. She held many of the same qualities and sharpness.

"Good God!" Arthur blurted. "What man agreed to that?"

Jeaneau calmly turned her head toward him. "A man worthy of my attention." She turned back to William and Mary. "My apologies, the subject has seemed to turn towards me. I believe your intention is to determine if I am reliable and honorable enough to complete your request. I am. If you did not already believe this, you would not have summoned me from across the Channel. I promise to make every attempt to safely deliver your guest to his new home. How do you wish to get him on my ship?"

"We will have him board with his entourage before the morning tide," William replied.

"Then I should have him in France by Christmas."

"My secretary will provide you with the number of guests boarding your ship and what provisions they will need."

"I could very likely carry no more than three or four passengers and conditions may not be up to their standards."

"I will ensure the number of guests is small. Provide what you can."

She nodded subserviently. "Then I request your leave, so I can prepare."

"Granted."

She curtsied once more and departed. Captain Edevane followed.

Arthur drank from his cup and said, "Told you she was brash. She'll not let James get the best of her."

"Perhaps a little too brash," Mary replied.

William looked up at his wife. "A woman of your position judging another strong woman?"

"My breeding gives me the right to such a will."

William returned to his table of papers and replied, "And her upbringing gives her that right. She is Dutch with a freewill. There are no laws stopping her from being a captain."

"I am sure Father will not like a woman sailing him to France."

"James has little say in the matter. He can sail to France or suffer a dire fate. I am sure he will choose exile by whatever means permitted."

Jeaneau listened to the door shut behind them and kept walking back down the long corridor. Her heart pounded in her chest as the reality of the moments before crashed in on her. She felt so calm and collected in the presence of royalty, but now, she felt all the panic and awe set in at once. She stopped for a moment, finding it hard to breathe, and felt a tremor in her hands.

Roger said something but it sounded distant in her ears. She turned to look at him. Her eyes were wide and her mouth slightly agape, but no sound emitted.

"Jeaneau," Roger asked again, "are you well?"

She closed her mouth and inhaled deeply. "Yes…" She shook her hands to stop the trembling. "Yes. I just…he got me so angry. I…was a bit blunt, wasn't I?"

He grinned softly. "A bit."

"Oh…" she said and began walking towards the exit. She shook her hands again and then wrung her fingers.

"I half expected you to dismiss him," he said with a nervous chuckle.

"I think I almost did." She returned the nervous laugh. "Oh!" She stopped suddenly. "I forgot to ask for terms!" She turned back to the door, unsure what to do.

"I will make sure they are submitted. I will simply let them know we negotiated them before your arrival."

She stared at him in relief. "Thank you."

He smiled. "You are welcome."

Jeaneau liked his smile. She lightly touched her palm retracing where his fingers touched. "Will you be accompanying us?"

"No," he said with regret. "I must return to my ship."

Her sadness was visible. "And I…must buy some English lace."

He nodded and lowered his gaze. "I hope he provides you the honor and respect you deserve."

Jeaneau knew to stand in this moment any longer would be dangerous. "Safe journeys, Captain."

He bowed. "And to you."

She watched him take his leave and absorbed each step into her memory. The sound of his boots on the stone. The swish of his coat, the knot in his hair and his distinct smell.

"You married Gustave," she told herself.

EIGHTEEN

In His Majesty's Service

"Who?" Jean-Pierre hissed.

"You heard me," Jeaneau replied while she changed.

"I just…that is rather difficult to fathom."

"Try contemplating it while standing in front of the future King of England." She slipped on her coat. "And that ass, Old man Smith, was there."

"The Lord Admiral," Jean-Pierre said with a snooty air.

"Yes, The Lord Admiral," she said in a mocking tone, "guzzling wine and not shutting up. I could see him just swaggering about making sure we all knew the whole plan was his idea. I'd like to see him appear so cocky while risking his ship." She checked her freshly bound hair in a mirror. "And the princess! Looking down at me for even thinking of sailing after marriage."

"You discussed your marriage with the future queen?" he asked in utter dismay.

"She brought it up."

*H*ours later Olav found her down in the hold, prepping beds. He rapped on a beam. "They are here."

She threw on her coat and frantically began to button it up. "How do you address a deposed King?"

"I don't even know how to address a posed King."

They hustled onto the main deck to assist their guests. In the shroud of night, a small boat sidled up to the side of the Daughter's Fortune. Jean-Pierre dropped the rope ladder and greeted the group, assisting them on board. The port was quiet with just the beginning stirrings of activity, so few took notice of the early boarders.

Jeaneau stood at the top with her arms behind her back, presenting herself as tall, open, but reserved. As they approached, she bowed at the waist like a man and motioned them aboard. She personally had no idea what The King looked like, so she waited for him to identify himself.

A small man stepped forward and looked up at her. "Captain." He motioned to a man behind him, who wore a wig of royal proportions and a face both swallow and weary. "His Excellency, King James II."

Jeaneau bowed again. "Welcome aboard. I have cleared my cabin for your use and rooms for your staff. Are there any women or children that need accommodation?"

"No, my family is already in France."

"If the winds favor us, then you will see them soon enough. May I ask how His Majesty, King James II, wishes to be addressed since we will be very close and rather informal on this trip."

"Your Majesty will be adequate enough," he said, already bored of the conversation and looking around.

"Then let me show you the ship and your quarters, Your Majesty."

bout an hour into the trip, The King staggered from Jeaneau's quarters and worked to hold onto anything. The ship was battling against the wind and water for every inch toward France and the fight was violent.

Jeaneau was pulling lines to adjust a sail.

"Captain," The King forced from his tight throat, "is there a storm?"

"No, Your Majesty."

"Then why are we being tossed about?"

"Because we are sailing the channel in the winter. Most ships have docked for the season, because sailing this time of the year is dangerous."

"Then he wishes me to perish?"

Jeaneau looked over her shoulder at The King and understood his meaning.

Of course, send The King on an unknown ship into the winter chop and let the sea take care of them both. No upstart captain to threaten their secrets and no king to challenge his throne. Death at sea would be a simple solution. Execution without consequence.

The rope jerked violently, forcing her focus back on her task. "Then he was a fool, Your Majesty."

James clutched to the stairs. "Why do you say that, Captain?"

"Because men always underestimate me." She grunted and secured the line.

The sea did not let up as they entered open water and the wind urged them towards the rocky coastline, but Jeaneau fought back, keeping the ship, slowly but surely, moving deeper into the waters and closer to France.

Her body started to give in to exhaustion. Slumping against the railing, she allowed another sailor to take his shift. Her muscles quivered and shook involuntarily, as she stumbled into her quarters to sit and take repast.

Pouring herself a glass of wine, she took off her wet scarf and pushed back the loose strands that had been whipped and jostled free from her braid. A soft grunt pushed past her lips when she took a bite of cheese. As she plopped into her chair, she heard a soft cough and quickly recalled her room was occupied.

"Your Majesty! My apologies." She stood and stepped towards the door.

The King put up a hand for her to remain. He lay in her bed, perhaps attempting to sleep, but was clearly awake. "This is an interesting room, Captain."

"Thank you?"

"It is a compliment. I just did not expect such a scholarly room, on a merchant ship." He brandished the latest book she was reading.

She remained quiet, unsure how to respond.

"You like to read?"

"Yes, Your Majesty."

"And invent?" He motioned towards her odd system of pipes that ran around the room.

"Yes," she replied.

His brow arched waiting for her to finish.

"Your Majesty."

He grinned in approval.

"Your Majesty?" she asked.

"Yes?"

"May I sit?"

"Sit?"

"Yes, I am quite exhausted and would like to rest. If you

wish to ask me further questions, then I simply ask for the opportunity to sit."

"Do you wish to sleep?"

"That was my plan, but I have made sleeping arrangements elsewhere. I simply came here out of habit."

"Very well then, you may leave to rest."

"Thank you, Your Majesty." She took a few items and started towards the door. Pausing, she asked, "Your Majesty, earlier you mentioned that Prince William wishes for you to die. Why did you say this?"

"As long as I live, I am a threat to his claim for the crown, even if he is given kingship, I can still contest his claim. If I am dead, the claim dies with me. Well, except for my son…"

"Then why not simply execute you?"

"These…Calvinists are odd. They choose the strangest times to be moral. To kill me outright would be murder. No, I need to die by accident. This exile is merely an excuse."

"So put you on a ship in the middle of winter and let Poseidon take you instead?"

"Precisely."

"And those that go down with you are of no consequence?"

"Why would they be?"

"And if I successfully get you to France? What then?"

"If I make it to France, then I should have enough allies to keep me safe as long as I have Louis's favor, but I doubt I will make it. Mark my words, an accident will happen."

She stood for a long moment, her head bowed in thought as she mulled over his words, then she lifted it and looked directly at him. "This room is very secure. Lock it behind me. You have my word, I will do everything in my power to ensure you make it to France."

NINETEEN

Duties and Favors

---

*J*eaneau rose Christmas morning and rolled out of her hammock. She could feel the ship continue to fight the waters. Sleep was short and sparse. Her body ached all over, but she ignored the pain and moved to the upper decks.

They were now approaching the coastline and the rocky shoals that lay beneath the crashing waves. Their timing was off so they had to fight the tide to maintain position but could not slip further down the coast until the tide shifted.

She ordered the anchor to be dropped and took this time to check and repair the ship. The small journey had already frayed the new ropes and the sails showed signs of stress tears.

The King and his small entourage took this time to come up top and survey the sea. Her sailors did their best to ignore their presence and repair the ship.

Jeaneau was up a mast fixing the rigging, when she glanced down and saw the King staring out to sea. She went back to work, but her head whipped around when she heard a yelp and then a splash.

Olav grabbed one of The King's entourages and she could see splashing in the water below.

Yanking at her skirt and tearing it off, she grabbed a rope. "Jean-Pierre, drop my bath!" She pushed off from the mast, until she was clear of the boat and close to the splashing figure, then let go.

She dropped into the water with great speed and quickly pushed herself to the surface. The water was brutally cold. Once her head broke free, she looked for the side of the boat, and then, using that as orientation, she looked for the body. Spotting heavily disturbed water and a head struggling to stay afloat, she headed toward it. Above them, her bath drop from its secure line into the water.

She swam toward the splashing and called out as she grabbed it from behind. He flailed and fought, but she pinned him against her and moved towards the box bobbing in the water.

"I need you to stop fighting," she shouted. "Relax your arms and kick your feet if you can."

The body submitted slightly but kicked her in the legs, repeatedly hindering her movement.

"Grab the box," she ordered, thrusting him against it.

He grabbed onto two of the many holes in the long rectangular container and continued to spit out water.

Grabbing the box, her numb fingers fumbled for the latch. She winced in pain but was able to open the hinged side. She pushed and pulled him into the chamber. "Stay inside," she ordered.

He moved and positioned himself inside, as she shut him in. Jeaneau pushed away from the contraption and shouted for it to be drawn up. As her bathhouse rose, the water drained from the multitude of holes, raining on her head. Wiping water from her eyes, she watched them secure the box against the ship where the captain's quarters were located.

She treaded water for a few moments trying to locate the expected rope ladder. She found it and swam. Climbing up the ladder, she returned to the deck dripping wet in her coat and hosen.

The crew did not find this strange, but The King's entourage gasped and murmured amongst themselves. She ignored this and approached Olav who was still holding a man.

She spoke through clenched teeth, trying to keep them from chattering. "What happened?"

"I saw him," Olav grunted. "He pushed The King over into the water."

She eyed the man. He stared back at her with no remorse.

Jeaneau grappled him, walked over to the railing, and pointed. "Do you see that coastline?"

The man fought back, but could not break her freakishly strong grip.

She pinned his arms behind his back. "I said, do you see that coastline?"

"Yes," he grunted back.

"Good, because swimming to it is your only chance to ever see land again." And before he could react, she lifted him off the deck and over the railing.

He screamed the whole way down.

"Raise the ladder." She ordered and walked to her quarters.

Inside, she found The King being undressed by Jean-Pierre and Lance. He shook and shivered.

Jeaneau grabbed her brandy and poured him a glass. She then went to her bed and grabbed her blankets, wrapping them around him.

"The man," The King stuttered.

"Dismissed," Jeaneau said coldly.

Jean-Pierre and Lance looked at her in grim shock, understanding her meaning.

Lance looked at Jeaneau. "You will need to change, too."

She began to strip, showing no indication of modesty. As the brandy and blankets warmed his body The King's body, he noticed her undressing. Not acknowledging his stares, she got into new clothes. Her one coat was soaked, so she rummaged for a replacement.

In her trunk, she found Edevane's coat and paused. Technically it was the coat of a British Naval Officer, currently under the new king, but nothing about it revealed this truth. She didn't care if he took offense to her wearing a man's coat under these circumstances. She decided warmth was more important and slipped on the coat.

The King sputtered softly, "Where did you get that?"

"From the second to last man I threw off my boat."

"Second to last?"

"Yes, I would say last, but since I just threw another off..."

The King looked baffled, but had little time to respond when there was a pounding on the door.

Jeaneau pulled open the peephole and saw Olav. "Yes?"

"The rest of His Majesty's party. They wish to know of his well-being."

"Inform them he is alive, then detain all of them."

"Yes, Captain."

"Why are you detaining my subjects?" The King blustered.

Jeaneau felt her adrenaline start to ebb and rubbed her head. "Because one of them tried to kill you."

"One of my men. Surely I thought it was one of your sailors."

"No, Olav saw the whole thing. It was one of your men. He has been dismissed, but who knows who else will try."

"You used that word again. What do you mean dismissed."

"I mean he is taking an alternate route to France. That is, if he can swim."

"How dare you deal with one of my subjects?"

"That subject tried to kill you," she snapped.

"You are not a king; you do not get to…"

She spun around and stared him directly in the eye, "I am the captain of this ship, I am the master of this domain, and you are no longer a king."

"I am King as long as I live and breathe!"

"And you live another day thanks to me. Now drink the brandy and stay in here until you are warm. I will have someone fetch a change of clothes from your trunks." She motioned to Jean-Pierre and Lance to follow her, leaving the king alone.

Lance followed her down to the hold. "Did you just yell at him?"

"He was being an ass."

"He's a king."

"Still an ass. I saved his life and he questions my actions. Should have let him drown." She stopped, feeling a wave of vertigo. Her knees buckled.

Lance reached out to steady her. "Captain, you need to lie down."

"We have work to do."

Lance walked Jeaneau over to the hammocks. "And it will be done. You may be able to order a king around, but in this case, I get to order you. Lay down."

Jeaneau slipped into one of the lower hammocks and was out in an instant.

She woke when Olav shook her shoulder softly and said, "Tides have changed."

Without delay, she moved topside, only detouring to her quarters to grab fresh gloves. There, she found the King still swaddled in blankets on her bed.

"Your Majesty," she said softly and moved to leave.

"Captain," The King called out through a pinched nose.

She hid an inner groan. "Yes, Your Majesty?"

"How much longer?"

"The tide has shifted, so we will attempt to bring the ship inland."

"Should I stay here?"

"It would be wisest." She turned and noticed he was holding a blood-soaked cloth to his nose. "Your Majesty!" she cried and instinctually lunged at him to assist.

He waved her back with his free hand. "A reoccurring malady."

"Should I fetch my surgeon?"

"No, it will pass." He pulled the cloth away to check the progress. "My people, they are still confined?"

"They are, but if you wish, you can lock the cabin behind me." She bowed in an attempt to leave.

But he spoke again. "You are Catholic?"

"I am."

"Is that why you rescued me?"

"I rescued His Majesty because I was asked to deliver you to France."

"So not out of loyalty or kindness?"

Her brow furrowed. "You are not my king or my friend."

"Even now in my deposed state, I still hold great power. Did this not occur to you?"

"No."

"Does it now?"

"It is known, but of little consequence. It is not in my nature to extort favors from an act of humanity."

"But favor, you could gain."

"If so, it will be given by choice, not by demand." She ran her fingers through her hair trying to calm her nerves. "I need to bring the ship in. Do I have the leave of His Majesty?"

He blotted his nose again and gave her a nod.

*J*eaneau watched from the upper deck as the king and his entourage departed the ship. Taking advantage of her position as captain, she stood at the helm to avoid a final conversation with His Majesty.

She watched Jean-Pierre converse with him before he went down the ramp and saw The King give him a letter. She was curious but did not move.

Once the entourage was gone and the gangway retracted, Jean-Pierre bounded up the stairs and stood at her side to watch. "Well," he said softly, "we didn't die."

She scoffed lightly. "Just barely and we still have to sail back out of this god forsaken bay and back up the coast."

"Well, at least you married a man with his own dock."

"I suppose this means I only have one man in one port."

He shrugged. "Such limitations never stopped most men."

She chuckled. "Do you not believe in the sanctity of marriage?"

He snorted. "Do you?"

She sniffed lightly. "Sanctity…no. Devotion, loyalty… when it is earned and given. Don't see it often."

"I have seen more than enough of this world that devotion in marriage has more to do with the measure of the man rather than any promise."

"Your cynicism is heartening."

"As is yours. The realities of life are harsh." He went to scratch his chin and remembered the letter. "From The King."

She took it. "Should I even read it?"

"He said use it if you ever wish to ask for that favor."

She slid it into the slit of her skirt and down into the pocket. When her hand came back out, it had a flask. Uncorking the top, she took a swig. "In the past six months, I have incidentally help overthrow a country and have met not one, but two kings. Oh, and got married."

Jean-Pierre took the flask and said, "Certainly a notable year. Merry Joyeux Noël, Mon Capitaine."

She wrapped an arm around his waist and leaned on his shoulder. "Merry Christmas, Jean-Pierre."

TWENTY

What the Tide Brings In

*R*oger held on as the small boat knocked up against Herbert's Flagship. He skillfully scaled the rope and headed to the captain's ready room, where he found other officers and the Lord Admiral leaning over a table, examining maps and reports.

He stepped in and bowed. "Lord Admiral."

"Roger, good. We are assigning winter posts. I'm sending you home."

"Sir?"

"We are going to be squabbling in parliament for some time, and by spring I suspect rebellion and pushback. I want you rested and ready."

"I appreciate the concern, but…"

"But nothing. Besides, I received word that your father is unclear about where his allegiances lay. Go home and sort things out. Make sure he knows his son's role in all this."

Roger nodded, understanding his true assignment. "Sir, you do know…"

Herbert waved dismissively. "Bastard or not, a word in the House of Lords can redeem or ruin him. Make sure he knows that."

"Yes, Lord Admiral."

"What have you done to my ship?" Gustave declared.

Jeaneau walked down the boarding ramp toward him. "Your ship?"

He motioned to the ship again. Gesturing at the ragged sails, worn ropes, and icy planks.

"I'm fully aware of her state. This is why we don't sail in the winter. But it is not your ship."

He took her hand and kissed her cheek in apology. "No, no. You are right. Our ship?"

Jeaneau softly grinned. "Then you will have no trouble bringing her back to glory."

His eyes narrowed slightly. "No…trouble, but?"

"But?" she asked, innocently raising her brows.

"Why do I sense you will be asking this as a favor and not paying."

Jeaneau put her hand delicately against his chest, and cooed. "But you said it was our ship."

He smirked, putting his arms around her. "Perhaps, we can discuss the terms after we get you out of these clothes?"

She coyly smiled. "Perhaps…"

Jeaneau gently stretched and started to slip out of bed when she felt a foot hook around her ankle.

"Do you ever sleep through the night?" Gustave softly mumbled.

"Not usually," she replied.

His hands reached out and gently slid her back into his arms.

She felt his warm naked body pressed against her flesh and her own form relented.

He kissed the back of her neck softly. "Something you may have to change."

"Do you sleep through the night?" she asked, her fingers trailing across his side.

"Usually. Though, if I do wake up after first sleep, I go back to bed. You, my dear, are as nocturnal as a bat."

"Agreed, the moon is my sun."

He shook his head softly. "I'm married to a creature of the night."

She laughed softly. "Whatever shall you do?"

"Wear you out?"

She looked over her shoulder at him. "Wear me out?"

He grinned broadly.

Olav did not get past his door before he found two curly haired toddlers in his arms. He kissed them both, then wriggled his head free enough to kiss their mother.

"What did you bring us?" Gertie asked.

"Yes, what did you bring?" Elsje begged.

Olav laughed. "You will see." He set them both down and dug into his bag, producing two small boxes. He put them before his girls. "Pick one."

Gertie and Elsje studied the boxes, then silently discussed, before each grabbing one. Each tore off the lid to find a beautiful doll inside.

"Baby!" Gertie declared and hugged it tightly.

"Oh, it is so pretty, Pater, thank you," Elsje declared and hugged his neck.

Gertie followed suit and nearly toppled a crouched Olav to the ground.

He caught himself and laughed. "Okay, go play!"

They adorned him with a shower of kisses and disappeared.

Olav stood and slipped his arms around his wife. "How long will that keep them distracted?"

"Eta will make sure it is long enough." She took his hand and drew him up the stairs. "Come, husband. Let's settle you in."

$\mathcal{M}$r. Wahl was standing on a ladder, reaching for a bottle, when the bell to his shop sounded as the door opened. He carefully cupped the jar in one arm and turned. His face broke into a smile when he saw his daughter. "Anna!" He descended the ladder with too much haste and began to fall.

Anna rushed to her father and kept him from hitting the floor. They laughed and embraced.

"I was beginning to worry I would not see you. You missed the festival of lights."

"I know, I am sorry. We had an unexpected delay, but I knew you would understand."

He studied her, from her covered head to her brown shoes, and assessed that she was well. "I understand, at least you made it before sunset. Go see your mother."

She kissed him softly on the cheek and entered the back room.

Her mother was tending to herbs in a sunny window, when she turned and saw her daughter. Overcome with joy, she nearly tipped a pot but caught it. Clutching herbs in one hand, she wrapped the other around Anna's neck. "You're home!"

They walked into the kitchen and immediately fell into sync to finish dinner for Sabbath.

"Why were you so delayed?"

"I told Papa that something unexpected came up, and it certainly did."

"Do tell."

Anna glanced at the door and could see, but not hear, her father upfront. Assured that their conversation was in secret, she leaned in. "We saved the King of England."

"What?!" her mother declared and then hushed herself.

"Have you heard news of what happened in England?"

"Oh yes, your father was quite concerned about what it would mean for your husband."

Anna nodded. "I am sure Mr. Pottinger will take little notice of the changing of the crown, especially since these new Christians do practice some tolerance, but Lance" –she checked the door again– "was on the ship that took the exiled King of England to France."

"No!" she said in awe.

"I personally prescribed him a tincture to help with his bloody nose."

Her mother put a hand to mouth in shock. "How did that happen?"

"We first had to get captured by the English/Dutch Fleet then escape. Then after the captain got married, we found ourselves back in England in December! I was getting on the coach when Jean-Pierre stopped me and said I was needed."

"Wait, your captain got married?"

"An ostentatious ship builder she uses for repairs. Surprised us all!"

"Oh Anna, I know why you are doing this, but it is so dangerous. What do we tell your father when you never come home?"

She stopped chopping, and clasped her mother's hand. "If that time comes, my captain will send word. I wish I could tell Papa, but…"

She nodded. "If he doesn't know, then he can't lie if you are found out."

"It's been 5 years. As far as his family knows, we died at sea."

"And as far as your father knows, you run the shop with him in England and come home to visit."

"Exactly."

She took in a breath to steady herself. "And come home you did. Now tell me more, before your father comes in to light the candles."

TWENTY-ONE

A Scot in Wales

*E*mmet tapped his finger on the table, as he stared at the parchment before him. He was oblivious to the raucous tavern life around him, trying to decide the name of the Dutch Naval Captain in his story. Sailing on a mainly Dutch ship, he knew several, but that was just the problem: giving this man a name that was not tied to a person that he knew or knew him.

He looked around the room seeking inspiration, but sadly, there were few Dutchmen in a Welsh tavern. Settling on Lisette for the heroine, he decided to make her a courier/spy and not a merchant captain, because that would be too obvious.

The story was coming along quite nicely, and he silently thanked his muses. Yet, if he wished to keep anyone from realizing that the characters were based on real people, he needed to come up with a good name for the naval captain.

"Rolf? No that has an R…hmmm." He pondered.

The sun shone directly in his face when the door opened, and he squinted. A shadowy figure filled the door frame and looked strangely familiar. As his eyes readjusted to the dimmer light, he noted the shadow was heading straight for him and the figure was Young Smith.

Emmet shuffled his papers, and shove them into his bag, before squeaking, "Young Smith!"

"Quartermaster." He bowed. "I thought that was you."

"Surprise," he weakly cheered, breaking out in a nervous sweat.

"Are you well?" Roger inquired, waiting for an invitation to sit.

"Me?" Emmet squawked. "I'm fine." He cleared his throat and lowered it an octave. "I'm fine."

"Do you live here?" Roger asked.

"No…no…I…do…not…ahem…live here."

"Visiting?"

"Yes, visiting. I…you see…it's the winter season, so the ship…is docked…"

Roger patiently waited for Emmet to finish.

"And…I…don't really…have a home…so…I…chose to stay…here…for the winter."

"I suppose Wales in the winter is better than Scotland."

"Oh! Yes, definitely!" Emmet blurted.

"The good news is I grew up here, so if there is any place, in particular, you would like to see, please let me know."

Emmet began to calm from the sudden encounter. "Thank you for the kind offer." He then noticed that Roger was still standing. "Oh! Sit, Smith sit."

Roger bowed again and took a seat. "My surname is actually Edevane."

"Oh…terribly sorry. We still call you Young Smith."

Roger smiled. "Quite all right. I liked being Young Smith."

"And you were liked," Emmet replied, as he quickly dug in his bag scribbling a note not to use any names with an E and fanned the ink dry.

"Was I interrupting something?"

"Oh! No…just wanted to write down something before I forgot." He tucked the paper away and capped the ink bottle. "So, you came home for Christmas?"

"No, I missed it."

"Too bad. What kept you?"

Roger gave Emmet a knowing look.

"Oh! Yes…right. I was already here."

Roger's head quirked. "So you did not sail with Captain Elricksen in December?"

Emmet was confused. "December?! The Captain avoids sailing in the winter season."

"Yes…" Roger mused. "She was requested to assist in a discreet manner."

Emmet edged closer and hushed his tone. "Is there something I missed?"

"I apologize. I feel I misspoke, and I am not able to say further."

Now Emmett was deeply curious, "Young Smith, did something happen between you and the Captain?"

Roger stiffened in surprise. He composed himself before speaking, "No, nothing involving me directly. I was simply… Perhaps we can speak of this in a more private venue. Do you have rooms?"

Emmet chuckled. "I have a room."

"I am rather frugal myself and have little more off-ship." Roger mulled over the situation.

"Your ship is here?"

"Yes, it has met up with the fleet on this side. I have time to visit family while we await orders."

Emmet was assessing the information provided and not provided, along with the current posts and gossip. "Does it have something to do with Herbert and a sudden trip to France?"

"The Lord Admiral Torrington?"

"Noooo, the other Herbert. George and his assistance in the sequestering of a mother and child."

Roger examined Emmet. "Strangely, yes and no."

Emmet nodded. "So I am getting warmer. I mentioned it because Wales and France do have a lot in common, as does Ireland, compared to the newest King. Is he King yet?"

Roger shifted slightly. "In all but name, but as I said, how the other safely escaped to France, I do not know. That was left to fate and Fortune."

Emmet caught Roger's emphasis on the word fortune and processed his meaning. "Oh!" He looked around. "Did they make it?"

Roger shook his head. "Unfortunately, I do not know. You will have to inform me once you return to the ship."

He placed his hand on the table. "Let us touch wood then to ensure there is a boat to meet me."

Roger touched the table. "Agreed. It would be a pity for a newly wedded bride to die so quickly."

"Bride?"

Roger became flustered. "Again, my apologies, of course, you do not know. When I saw your captain, she had just recently wed."

"Who?!" Emmet squawked.

"A Mr. Oostwal. Ship builder I believe."

"Gustave? Jeaneau married Gustave!"

TWENTY-TWO

Raise the Flag

(TW: Martial Fighting, mild violence.)

As the dawn broke, Jeaneau woke, and this time successfully escaped Gustave's bed and chambers. The *wearing out* was clearly a mutual exchange.

She stepped into the hall, seeking out the morning sun. It was a personal pleasure because the gentle winter light did not burn her skin. She could hear the staff busy at work, preparing breakfast and letting in the light. While it did not compete with the soft rapping sounds of sails and rope knocking in the wind, it was pleasant.

Not wanting to disturb them, she slipped into the study, pulled back the curtains, and opened the large window. Inhaling in the cold wet air, she welcomed the morning mist.

Despite her best efforts, the housekeeper had spied her exit and entered the study with a tea tray. They exchanged silent good tidings and Jeaneau was left to bask in the light.

She pulled a small vial from her dressing gown and sprinkled tiny seeds into her hand. Popping the seeding into her mouth, she sipped the perfectly warm bitter liquid and sighed in bliss.

The steward stepped in with morning missives, including one from her mother.

She politely took the letter and tapped it against her mouth. Before even opening it, she knew it likely contained instructions and directions for the upcoming ceremony. Getting married would not stop her mother from having an extravagant event.

Jeaneau was shocked at how well her mother was handling the nuptials. Her only insistence was an official ceremony in France. Alas, she would need to read the correspondence. Reluctantly rising from her seat, she walked over to the desk in search of the letter opener.

She rummaged around Gustave's desk, which like her own, appeared disorganized and untidy. Yet, she knew that there was likely a method to this apparent chaos.

She tried to be careful in lifting stacks and moving aside scrolls in a desperate attempt to find the knife, but utterly failed when a stack toppled to the ground. Sighing, she bent down to clean it up.

As she reorganized the papers, she noticed her mother's handwriting and wondered what it was. Perhaps her mother was more upset than she realized and had written Gustave. Concern that her mother had said something untoward to her new husband, won out over any propriety or discretion. She read the letter, then she read it again. All color drained from her face, and she sat down on the floor in disbelief.

"Jeaneau," Gustave called out as he entered the study. "Jeaneau?" he said again, not immediately seeing her.

She carefully stood up and held his gaze.

"Jeaneau, are you well? What are you doing down there?"

She lifted the letter for him to see.

He approached in concern. "What is it, Dearest? Bad news? Is someone ill?"

She walked away from him. "I may be."

"Are you ill?"

She bent over in anguish, but it was not a cold that plagued her. "You tricked me."

"Tricked you?" he replied, completely baffled.

"You!" she said, her fury rising. "You duped me into marrying you!"

"What?" He reached out for her.

She pushed him away, and brandished the letter. "My mother told you to ask for my hand!"

He looked at her with shock and paused to calculate his next words. "Dearest."

"Don't Dearest me. She promised you alliances and stock! Building a warehouse here was her idea!"

His hands dropped to his side "Yes…"

She bent over again, unable to hold back her sobs. "How could you?! You know how I feel about being sold off."

He reached out again, and this time pinned her arms down, pulling her close. "I did it because I wanted you."

She stomped on his foot, forcing him to break his hold. Fleeing from him, she spat, "Because you wanted me, it was okay to buy me?"

"I didn't buy you, Jeaneau!" he yelled back and chased her about the room.

"Yes, you did! You get me, and a tidy little bonus of political and physical gains. Congratulations!"

"Damn it, Jeaneau! Stop!" he said and pushed her against the drawn curtains. He wrapped the ties around her wrists and kept her pinned. He ignored her kicks and attempts to bite and waited for her to calm down.

She stopped fighting but did not look at him.

Sternly, he said, "I did not marry you because your mother told me to, or what she promised. I didn't ask for your hand from your mother or father. I asked for it from you."

"After they gave their blessing!"

He scoffed. "Isn't that how it is supposed to work?"

She huffed and tried to wriggle free.

Keeping her pinned, he brushed her hot tears away with one hand.

"Did you actually ask them?" she inquired.

He nodded, playing with her wild hair. "I did, but unlike your other suitors, you actually reciprocate my feelings."

She looked at him coldly. "Who says I do?"

"Then who is actually using who?"

She glanced away.

He pulled her gaze back to him. "Use me, Jeaneau. Use me to make your business stronger." He unwound her hands and slipped his own around her. "Use me, so your mother can't use you."

"But she…"

"No," came a muffled reply as he gently kissed her neck. "We beat her at her own game."

She flinched, still upset. He held her in place and bit down. The sensation sent shivers across her body.

Jeaneau's anger ebbed as his hands ran across her sides and his hot breath trailed down her chest. He caressed and cajoled her body to relax. She knew what he wanted, but he also wanted her to relent. To give in and forgive him.

Could she forgive him? Could she push aside that he conspired with her mother? How could she not forgive him? Perhaps she was overreacting, dowry was always on the table. She just never thought he'd take it.

"Why?" she asked. "Why did you take the offer?"

He pulled his head out of her hair. "Honestly? To save your reputation."

"What?"

"You did run away."

"I'm a grown woman. I left."

He put his fingers gently on her lips. "You were an unmarried woman who left her mother's estate and suddenly married a foreigner."

"I. Well…" she tried to argue.

He softly shook his head. "Contingency contracts were in place. Imagine your father informing people that you married, and your new husband was getting nothing. What scandals would ensue? What litigation?"

She looked down knowing he was right. Sudden marriages often entailed a scandalous reason; pregnancy, upholding honor, avoiding destitution.

"You wanted a way to subvert your mother and have some free will in choosing who you married." He stepped slightly away from her and presented himself. "I provided."

She lowered her gaze, ashamed of her outburst.

He scooped her hands into his and guided her to sit on the open windowsill, then gazed deeply into her eyes. "Use me." Nudging her knees, he stepped between her legs. Neither broke eye contact.

She could see and feel his lust. His desire.

He kept her gaze, lowering his lips to hers and repeated, "Use me."

Forgiveness would not come without proof. Physical proof.

She unknotted the tie of his dressing gown and drew it open.

She felt like a goddess in his arms. A gift that he worshiped and devoured. How could a man act in this way if he did not love her, want her? The world froze for a moment, then the two collapsed to the floor a twisted broken mess.

Gustave huffed, "You will be the death of me."

"Will I?" she asked, trying to catch her own breath.

"Aye, but well worth the ride. Perhaps your goal is to send me to my grave."

She smacked him lightly. "It is not," she replied and moved to sit up. Wincing, she could feel the bruises developing on her hips and saw the scratch marks along her body as she closed her robe.

"I won't fight," he responded. "I will go willingly if it is by this path."

"Gustave, stop," she chided him.

"Yes, My Mistress," he said as he pulled himself off the floor. "I do your bidding."

She chagrined and shook her head.

As he stood, he pulled something stuck to his leg. It was an unopened letter from her mother. "Is this what started all of this?" he asked.

She pulled herself into a chair and reached for her now cold tea. "Indirectly, yes. I was looking for the letter opener."

"Ah," he replied, reaching over and grabbing it.

She was correct, just like her quarters. Organized madness.

TWENTY-THREE

Repositioning

---

*R*oger stopped briefly before crossing the gates to his childhood home. The memories were bitter and sweet. Filled with moments of rolling down hills and chasing rabbits, but also sad realizations that he would never be equal to his own blood, both in adoration and recognition. All of this molded him into the man he was now, someone who believed in conviction, loyalty, honesty, and being forthright. He steadied his thoughts and moved forward.

Arriving at the house, he did not enter the front door but moved to the back of the estate where smoke softly billowed out of a chimney pipe. He dodged the roaming chickens and stepped through the kitchen door.

Inside his mother stoked a fire under a boiling pot. He stole a moment to watch her move about the kitchen and softly order the rest of the staff.

He inhaled the scent of a fine roast, and by the smell of caramelized onions, it was nearly done. "Fanny, I would pull the beast before my mother yells at you."

The staff members tossed quick glances without breaking their rhythm and let out a cheer of Hello. Fanny let out a surprised start, smiled, and rushed to the oven.

A beaming smile broke across his mother's face, and she rushed towards him. "Roger!"

Smiling back, he swooped her into his arms. "Hello, Mam."

She pulled out of the hug and examined him. "Are you well?"

He chuckled. "Yes, I am well."

She eyed him suspiciously.

"Truly, I am fine."

"You are definitely too thin, and your cheeks are sallow."

He smiled softly. "Would you care to remedy that?"

"Of course!"

She silently ordered someone to fetch a chair, and before he was seated, a full meal lay before him. Fanny handed him a cup of ale and blushed. He returned with a polite smile and thanks.

"Why are you home so late?! I feared you'd dead!" his mother said, already back at her station and stirring a pot.

"Surely you know what happened."

"I do, but did I get a letter from you? No, I had to hear it from Eustis."

"I did send you a letter."

"Back in November, but nothing since."

"You are correct. I am sorry for not writing. Communication was limited and I became preoccupied." He took another bite. "Would you care for me to write now? Dear Mam, I am well, but this chicken is dry."

A spoon clanged loudly, and he burst out laughing at the sight of his mother's face. The rest of the staff joined his laughter but quickly ceased with one look from her.

"Do not lie to me and tell me that my chicken is dry, just to make me angry and forget all my worry these past two months." She picked up her spoon and went back to stirring.

Standing, Roger walked over to his mother and curled his arms around her shoulders. She calmed under his embrace.

He gently kissed the top of her cloth wrapped head. "I am sorry."

"Ie, you are," she replied and smacked his hand with her spoon. "Now go find Eustis, so he can prep you a bed upstairs."

He leaned down and kissed her cheek. "Ie, Mam." Before he left, he took a few more bites of food and drink, then asked, "Is He home?"

"Yes, he should be in his study."

He walked up the stairs into the main house and found Eustis.

Eustis gave him a familial hug and immediately offered to set up a bed. "How long are you staying?"

"Just for the night. I have quarters arranged in town. I need to be closer to the port."

"Nonsense. You should stay here. Especially since..." Eustis cut himself off.

"Since?" Roger asked.

Eustis hesitated. "I think you should speak to the Master."

Roger was curious and concerned. He could see the color drain from Eustis's face and his demeanor sullen. "Is everything well?"

"Come, he is in the study."

Roger was escorted to the master's study. The room was little changed from his youth, though certainly smaller, now that he was not crawling on the floor, playing soldiers with Peter.

The Master of the House, his father, sat at his table working.

He looked up when Eustis entered the room and made eye contact with Roger. "You are home."

He bowed. "Yes, Lord Garrick."

"Have you seen your mother?"

"First thing."

"Good. She was ready to demand word from the new king himself if she did not hear from you soon."

"My apologies. I was awaiting orders."

"And they were to come home?"

"I have joined a fleet on this side."

"Ah, yes. Need to keep an eye on those savages."

His father referred to the Irish, but they both knew that Wales was also heavily Catholic and would side with the dethroned king. Including the Earl of Powis, a friend of his father's.

"Do not look at me like that," he snapped. "None should be surprised that George helped Mary. It's the Catholics that fear persecution here."

"At least the exchange was bloodless," Roger offered.

"Bloodless!" Lord Garrick exclaimed. "Maybe no king died, but it was not bloodless."

Roger's brow furrowed.

"My Lord. I have not told him," Eustis interjected.

"Told me what?"

Lord Garrick's anger crumbled into deep sadness, as he slumped back into his chair.

Eustis looked at Roger directly and softly spoke. "Peter…"

"Peter?"

"There was an altercation in town. Peter-" Eustis' voice failed him.

Roger paled. The aura of the room spoke for them. Peter was dead. His half-brother, heir to the house, was dead.

"I…I am sorry," Roger stuttered.

Lord Garrick dismissed his apology with a wave of his hand. "It is done." He straightened, but did not make eye contact. "Come to dinner this evening. We will have much to discuss. Eustis, prepare him quarters in one of the guest rooms."

"Of course, My Lord."

*J*eaneau rocked back and forth on her feet as she stood on the pedestal.

The draper desperately worked to make an even hem, despite the constant movement.

"Jeaneau!" her mother snapped. "Please stand still."

She sighed and pushed back loose strands of hair, then squared her feet.

"Feet together, please. You are not some guard holding back a horde. You are a flower, slender and delicate."

Jean-Pierre stifled a snorting laugh, then swallowed hard when the gaze of Jeaneau's mother fell on him.

Jeaneau smirked. "Mother, how much longer? I feel as though I have stood here forever."

"Perfection requires patience."

Jeaneau looked down and could see that draper had made a full revolution around her and was sticking in the last pin to the hem. The minute it was done she wriggled out of the skirt without permission, then began to fuss with getting out of her bodice. She stopped when she heard something tear and the draper gasped. Dropping her hands in defeat, she waited for the flurry of attendants to release her.

Once the bodice was off, her mother and the draper fussed over the garment, searching for the tear.

Jeaneau plopped onto the couch and into Jean-Pierre's lap. "Take me away from all of this," she said in an overly dramatic fashion.

He stared down at her. "You agreed to marriage."

She rubbed her brow and grumbled, "But I am married, so why do I need an actual wedding?"

"But one must have a wedding in the spring!" Jean-Pierre jested.

She tried to sink further into the couch. "Then call me in the summer when it is done." She glanced over at her mother, still entrenched in discussing seams and finishing touches, then back to Jean-Pierre. "I bet we can sneak out."

"And go where?"

"Anywhere but here."

They both stealthily lifted off the couch and moved toward the door. She got them out the door and down the stairs before she heard her mother's voice calling. Shoving Jean-Pierre into Gustav's study, she quickly shut the door.

"Jeaneau, this is his study."

"And?" She found the decanters and poured them drinks. "She certainly won't look here." She handed him a drink. "When do we sail next?"

"We?"

"Yes, we. I was promised I could keep sailing, so I don't plan on stopping."

"Well, we have little to do till the waters calm and the ceremony, and I assume a trip with your new husband."

She took a sip. "Good God, all that. Can't he just come with us?"

Jean-Pierre scratched his head. "I suppose. Your quarters may be a bit confined for him. But do you want him to?"

She frowned and played with her glass. "I think he will be too great a…distraction."

Jean-Pierre snorted. "A little too demanding of your time."

Jeaneau slumped into the chair. "It will be nice to not be so…adored."

Jean-Pierre glanced at her neck sprinkled with love bites. "Is that what you call it?"

She rolled her eyes at him knowing the same argument was about to start again. "We do talk, Jean-Pierre."

She looked away from him, hoping her reply was enough, and rummaged through the papers on the table. She saw the old report on Louis' hold in the Rhinelands, next to it a letter with a royal French seal. Picking it up, she read it, then let out an astonished laugh. "My mother is going to love this."

"What?" Jean-Pierre replied.

"Louis is offering Gustav a position. My mother's dream come true. I will become one of the bourgeois." She threw the paper down and poured another glass.

"Jeaneau?"

"All of it." She seethed. "Everything I tried to avoid is happening. Sold and used to gain favor."

"I did ask…" Jean-Pierre said softly and stepped beside her.

She leaned on his shoulder. "I know."

"Are you okay?"

"I…" she sighed, "I just need time to adjust."

"Should you have to?"

"That is what marriage is, right? Adjustment? Compromise?"

He shrugged. "I wouldn't know."

"I'll be better once we are at sea again."

"Sans Gustave?"

"Definitely no Gustave."

TWENTY-FOUR

Broadsided

Roger sat on the bench in the guest room and buttoned his vest. He never had his own bed in this house, before he left for the sea, simply sharing one with his mother. Though many a night, she did not sleep in it.

Going from a tiny bed crammed in a corner to a room, bigger than his Captain's Cabin, the sheer size and opulence of the room was more than he desired. The gesture and implications were clear. Lord Garrick wanted something.

His relationship with his father was convoluted at best. He could never call him that. For a long time, he didn't even know that Lord Garrick was his father. He and Peter were close in age and played together as siblings, neither knowing the truth. It was not until Peter's cousin shoved Roger to the ground and spat the word bastard at him, that he even questioned his lineage.

He was the son of the cook. He didn't need a father. He had Eustis and the other male servants like the stableman, who taught him how to ride and hammer metal into nails.

The day his mother told him was also the day she told him he was leaving. That he was going to learn to sail and maybe someday captain a vessel.

He stood to fasten the last few buttons and looked in the mirror. Here he was, captain of a ship, dressed in fine, but sensible clothes, fitting for a man of good standing and yet still a bastard. Putting on his coat, he walked downstairs to the dining room. There were only two place settings.

He lingered in the doorway. Their first time officially sitting at the table and they would dine alone? He wondered how lonely Lord Garrick must be now. No son, no wife, no other children.

While waiting for Lord Garrick to arrive, he walked over to his place setting.

Lord Garrick entered the room. A servant pulled out his chair and he sat.

Roger waited for the servant and then sat as well.

Dinner was served and they ate in silence. Roger knew not to speak until permitted.

"Your manners are admirable," Lord Garrick finally said.

He finished sipping his soup and set down his spoon. "I was taught to match the decorum of the event. This is the house of a lord."

Lord Garrick nodded. "And your schooling? How well do you read and write?"

"I would consider myself adequate."

He sipped. "I'm told sailors often know other languages."

Roger replied, "I do. I can read and speak in Spanish and English. I picked up Latin to better understand the Mediterranean countries."

Lord Garrick looked at him with surprised admiration. "Truly." He blotted his mouth. "That is where your last campaign was before…"

"Yes, I was under Lord Torrington as a Lt."

He snorted. "The now Lord High Admiral Torrington. How is the pompous ass?"

"Still pompous," Roger replied. "But also sharp as a knife."

"Your mother mentioned you were in The Fleet from Amsterdam."

"I was."

"And a captain now."

"Yes, sir."

"Tell me, have you met the new King?"

Roger paused. "Yes."

"Are you in his favor?"

Roger had to willfully keep himself from shifting due to discomfort, and needed to be careful with his words. "I can not directly confirm such an opinion, but I see no reason that I am in his disfavor."

He took another sip. "Well there is that."

"Do you like being in the Navy?"

"It…yes."

Lord Garrick swirled the wine in his cup and studied him.

Roger inhaled. "It is a challenge and not what I would have chosen, but I do enjoy life at sea."

"Really?" he inquired.

"I've seen the world. Learned new languages, visited wonders, and met a plethora of diversity." His appreciation for the experience was evident in his voice.

"Ah, much like taking The Grand Tour?"

Roger nodded. "Yes, I imagine it is similar."

The soups were taken away and the main course was provided.

Lord Garrick did not pick up his fork, so Roger waited.

Instead, Lord Garrick stared at Roger for a long time and then said, "Roger, do you know why you are here?"

"Here? As in Wales?"

"No, here. As in this table, right now."

Roger adjusted his poster slightly. "I have my guesses, but will not make any assumptions."

He tapped his fork lightly. "With Peter's loss and Allison never able to bear another child before she died…" He exhaled. "I am sure it was the fever that came over her that one winter." His eyes met Roger's. "This has left me no legitimate heirs."

Roger pushed down years of rejection and maintained his composure. "You could marry again. I am sure a young wife can bear you many future sons."

Lord Garrick eyed him keenly. "I could, but…"

Roger returned his stare and waited.

Regret in his tone, he spoke. "I can not do that to your mother twice."

Roger failed to hide the shock on his face. "Twice?"

The mask of a master slowly melted away from Lord Garrick's face.

Roger began to see a mere man sitting there. A man who was suffering from great loss and forced to face the deeper truths of the world.

"I am not sure how to say this or where to begin."

"What do you mean twice?" Roger asked again.

"How old are you now?"

"Nearly Four and Twenty."

He nodded. "I was about your age, perhaps younger when I fell in love with your mother. She was barely a cook's assistant then. I was enamored. Her skin, so dark, and her eyes." He lingered a moment in the memory. "But I was a nobleman's son and my marriage was already arranged. Truly, Alison had no care for the arrangement either, but family obligations and…" He stopped and took a sip of his wine. "Despite being married I could not stop loving your mother and Alison did not stop it." He chuckled. "She even said once that as long as it kept me out of her bed, she did not care."

Roger was frozen. He sat and stared as Lord Garrick revealed unspoken history.

"Then you came. We were careful, but The Fates cast their dice in your favor."

Roger was not sure he agreed with that.

"Alison was livid. She was already pregnant with Peter. I even suggested claiming you as hers. Twins is all anyone outside the house would have known, but alas you looked just enough like your mother, the farce would not have lasted. And your mother!" He chuckled at the memory. "She nearly pushed me off the balcony when I suggested it." He tipped his glass at Roger. "And let me tell you, when you have two women ready to kill you, you do as they wish."

Roger noticed his throat was parched, so with great care, he picked up his own glass and took a sip. "So instead you kept on my mother and just let me think I had lost a father to the war?"

"Easy enough lie for a small child and town."

"Until I found out."

Lord Garrick let out a long sigh and shook his head. "Cedric."

Roger nodded.

"By that time you were old enough that you would have realized." He regretfully sighed. "And then there was the matter of your education. I could not send you to school with Peter. The best solution was the Navy. I commissioned you to be trained as an officer, which meant receiving an education and securing your future. It was the best I could do."

Roger was still struggling with revelations and years of resentment, but politely replied, "And I appreciate the opportunity."

"Bah!" Lord Garrick said, the wine seeping into his blood. "I was a coward, and your mother never forgave me!" He started to blubber. "Even now, she refuses me, and I"–he motioned to the empty room–"I have nothing."

Roger watched him crumble into full sobs.

Lord Garrick choked back his tears. "Not even you. I wanted to ask you to be my son, but...I can see it. You do not want me as your father."

Roger observed him for a long time, unable to fully

express the quagmire of thoughts and emotions pressing against his chest. He stayed silent until Lord Garrick stopped crying and regained his composure, then spoke.

"You are my father by blood, but it is you who did not acknowledge me. I've always wanted you as my father. To love me, as you loved Peter. But you never showed me any fatherly affection or guidance. Luckily, there were other men that filled that void, including Eustis and Arthur. But I forgave you for that long ago."

A moment of hope sparked in Lord Garrick's eyes.

Roger stood up, forcing the chair to loudly slide back. "But what you did to my mother." He threw his napkin on the table. "I don't think I can ever forgive that."

Lord Garrick grabbed his wrist. "Wait! No, no, you are right. What I did to her. What I have done to her was wrong and unjust. I am trying to make it up to her now."

"How?" Roger seethed.

"By officially declaring you my son and heir."

Roger glared at him. "Then marry her."

"What?"

"Marry her and then, by default, you can claim me as your heir."

"I would, but she will not marry me." His voice quivered. "Too much bad blood."

Roger pulled his arm free. "If she will not have you, then I will not," he declared, curtly bowed and left.

*E*mmet put away his papers and took the last draught from his mug. As he started to climb the stairs to his room, he caught the glint of a familiar coat entering the inn.

It was Roger and despite appearing calm and composed, Emmet knew something was wrong.

He turned and called out, "Young Smith, I did not expect to see you at this late hour."

Roger froze, calculating his answer.

Emmet relieved him of this task by blurting, "Good night beer! I mean…have a beer…have a good night beer with me."

Roger softly bowed. "Obliged."

Emmet shuffled his satchel to one side and awkwardly hooked his arm around Roger's. They walked over to a corner table and sat.

The innkeeper, completely unable to not hear the bizarre conversation, was already en route with drinks. "Here you are," she said politely flashing a smile. "I saw you earlier today. Are you Adah's son?"

Roger swallowed, working to stay collected. "Yes."

"Welcome home then. First drink is on me. Sorry about Peter."

Emmet's eyes darted back and forth between the exchange but remained quiet.

Roger picked up his drink and sipped.

Emmet knew this look. This was the look of a deeply troubled man. To see it on Roger was strange. Especially since his mood was different hours before.

"Have you eaten?" Emmet asked.

"Yes," Roger began. "No…not really."

"Then we should eat. No need to go to bed on an empty stomach."

"I thought you were heading up to sleep."

"Sleep?" he chirped. "Nonono, stare at the ceiling for a few hours, most likely. Besides, I can always eat."

Emmet ordered full meals for them both, already aware of the best dishes the inn provided.

Roger ate and drank, his shoulders softened and he started to relax.

"Your mother's name is Adah?" Emmet inquired.

Roger nodded.

"And she lives here?" Emmet asked, trying to remember the steps to polite conversation.

"She does. She is a local Landed Lord's Cook."

Emmet blinked at the bitterness that stuck to Roger's last word. He fidgeted. "Is he a bad lord?"

Roger put down his fork and scowled out the window. "No."

"I'm awfully terrible at these sorts of things and it is no business of mine on the matter, but you do seem immensely upset. Has something bad happened?"

Roger gazed at Emmet with sad, but apologetic eyes. "I am sorry if my sullen demeanor has caused you distress. I am also not adequately attuned to communicating matters of the heart."

"Heart?" Emmet leaned in closer. "Have you been scorned?" His eyes twinkled with anticipation.

Roger thought for a moment. "In a way, it is that I believe…I think I have been un…scorned."

"Indeed?" Emmet asked, elated. "Who scorned you in the past to now make recompense?"

Roger's fork swirled around on his plate. "My father."

This was not the person Emmet expected him to say. He was hoping for some delectable tale of a first love, who had left him for another. Or perhaps an unrequited romance. Since the moment he saw Roger again, he truly hoped that the man would confide in him an unspoken affection for Jeaneau and divulge any romantic exchanges. Anything to spice up his writing.

He and Olav had a running bet against Jean-Pierre, who swore nothing happened. To prove Jean-Pierre wrong would be delicious. Alas, if there was something, this was not the moment of truth.

Instead, Emmet replied, "A father's scorn. I know that well."

"Does he not approve of you being a sailor?"

"Ha!" Emmet blurted. "If he even knew, I would doubt he'd care."

"You left home without his approval?"

"Roger," Emmet said very seriously, "I ran!"

"And never looked back?"

"Not even a second."

"Perhaps I should have considered that."

"But your mother is alive and here."

Roger agreed and took another drink. "And your mother?"

"Dead and gone. Leaving me to take care of his drunken ass as a good daughter should," Emmet said without thinking.

Roger caught the discrepancy, but let it pass.

"I am sorry for your loss."

Emmet brushed off the condolence. "Years ago."

"What did you do when you ran away?"

Emmet beamed. "I became an attorney."

Roger's interest was piqued. "An attorney?"

"Yes…once I left home, I got hired as a clerk and earned my right to practice."

"How does an attorney end up on a ship?"

"Well…" Emmet replied, rocking slightly in his seat. "Funny story. I met Jean-Pierre and Olav one night when I found them dangling a man off a dock."

"A dock?"

He took a sip. "Mmhmm, apparently it was their former purser who they discovered was…making special stipulations in the ship's contracts that were…unbalanced."

"Ah, I see."

"I negotiated that, in return for them not dropping the poor soul in the drink, I could take a look at the contracts, and if there was foul play, we could sue for recompense."

"And did you?"

"Didn't even get that far. While I was going over the contracts the rat fled the ship never to be seen again."

"But how did you end up the Quartermaster?"

"Olav and Jean-Pierre got me very drunk and convinced me to work for them. The Clerk's office is a dreadfully dull place. I had never gone farther than my home to there. The whole point of running away was to live, so I did."

"Not many people willingly choose the sea. I am sure you could be settled and with a family by now if you'd stayed."

Emmet shuddered and took another drink. "Last thing I wish is to be settled. Besides, I do have a family and one that doesn't expect me to get married and have kids."

"Sailors are not cut from the same cloth as other men, but your ship in particular."

"Is a rarity indeed," Emmet blurted. "It is what makes her special."

"How did Captain Elricksen become a captain? She told me she was raised on a ship, but…"

"Claude!" Emmet blasted.

The innkeeper shushed him.

He gave her a bobbing nod, then softly said, "Claude."

"Her brother?"

Emmet nodded. "He and Jeaneau helped their father run the company and co-captained a ship when they were 18! But then Claude decides he doesn't want to stay within the law and starts smuggling. He gets caught and nearly does the business in. But Jeaneau and her father were able to make some arrangements to get him out of jail." He stabbed a potato and waggled it at Roger. "But then he disappears." Emmet leaned in closer. "It's said he's a pirate. Don't mention him or pirates around Jeaneau. Claude's actions nearly done them in, but she's savvy and not only got the charges dropped but established new contracts."

"I've seen her at work," he concurred and took another

sip. "So, she and Claude Co-Captained the Daughter's Fortune?"

Emmet's head sloshed. "No, no. The ship was a gift. Her father had it built just for her. That's why it is called Daughter's Fortune. A gift to her, to make her own fortune."

"Impressive. At least someone has a good relationship with their father."

Emmet laughed. "It's quite an envy to see. They adore each other, support each other and weather that mother of hers!"

"Her mother?"

"Frightening woman, in the very best sense. Shrewd and socially brilliant. She could talk a man out of his clothes in a blizzard."

Roger looked at Emmet quizzically.

"No…not like that. Make him give her his clothes."

Roger gave an unsure nod.

"Fathers!" Emmet blurted. "We were talking about fathers. Mine is a sot. Yours?"

Roger took another large gulp of ale and hesitated to speak.

"Come, come," he softly beckoned. "You clearly need to talk to someone. I don't live here, so talk to me. What did your father do?"

"He…he asked me to be his son."

Emmet paused, trying to process the statement. "Aren't you already his son? I mean you are a man, right?"

Roger nodded. "I am not his legitimate child. He has never claimed me."

Emmet released a barely audible, "Oh…" He scratched the back of his ear and motioned for Roger to explain.

"His heir just died. Peter."

"So that would make Peter your brother and…oh no… and he just out of nowhere asked you to be his heir?"

Roger confirmed and took another drink.

"Did you know Peter?"

"I did. We grew up together and stayed in touch. He just finished his Grand Tour. I didn't even know he was home."

He took another sip. "So, this bastard!"

"No, I'm the bastard," Roger mumbled.

"No! No," Emmet said, brandishing a finger. "Fine. That braggart, just ups and expects you to say yes after losing your brother. And your mother, what is she to him?"

"She's his cook."

"The landed lord?! That's your father? Young Smith, you are holding out on me."

Roger's head slunk. "I told him no."

"Good for you!"

Roger lifted his head in surprise.

"What has he done for you?"

"He did pay for my commission."

"Bah, hush money and probably expected you to die at sea."

"He says he still loves my mother."

"Then why doesn't he marry her?"

"That's what I said!" Roger blurted.

"Enough of this. You deserve to get drunk." Emmet motioned to the innkeeper. "Brother dead, Father a cowardly ass, with the audacity to ask you to take on his estate. What does he expect you to do? Leave the Navy?"

"I don't know if I can."

"Right? There is a war coming."

The innkeeper came over and put down a flagon. "Took you long enough. Drink, but no brawling."

Emmet encouraged Roger to drink and would randomly break out into song. He persuaded Roger and other late-night patrons to join. It took a good amount of alcohol to get Roger smiling and by the time the innkeeper cleared the tables, he threw Roger's arm over his shoulder and helped him up the stairs. There, with trained skill, he got

Roger into the bed, boots off, and then he slumped into a chair.

The next morning Emmet walked down from his room and fetched breakfast. Balanced on a tray were sausage, potatoes, eggs, and a pot of hot coffee. Deftly using mainly his feet, he got the door open and the tray onto the small table.

He sat and waited. Having dealt with many drunk men, he knew the best way to not startle them was to act like you'd always been there.

Roger stirred and lifted his head. He noticed a cup still clutched in his hand and dropped it.

"Probably best," said Emmet.

Roger looked in his direction, but his eyes would not focus. "Hylo?"

Emmet smirked, hearing Roger speaking with an accent. He knew Roger's good English was a ruse. Emmet's own accent came out when he was tired or drunk.

"Good morning, Young Smith."

"Emmet?"

He nodded and picked up the fallen cup.

Roger sat up slowly, rubbed his face, and took in a deep breath.

Emmet watched Roger turn green upon smelling the food. With one foot, he hooked and slid the piss bucket right between Roger's feet.

Roger hurled up last night's imbibement, then forced himself into an upright position.

Emmet handed him a handkerchief and a cup of child's beer. "Rinse, spit, then wipe your mouth."

Roger complied. Rubbing his face, he looked around the small room. It was a scattered mess, papers and clothes strewn about, vastly different from the meticulously organized ship's hold.

Emmet picked up the tray and put it on the bed. He snagged a sausage and began eating silently.

Eventually, Roger took a few gentle sips of coffee and picked up his fork.

The silence lasted until Emmet could see Roger's color return.

Emmet drank his own coffee. "I did not take you for someone who drinks until they pass out."

Roger kept his eyes lowered in shame. "I am not."

"Not to worry then, getting a few sheets to the wind once or twice does not a drunk make. Trust me, you could be much worse."

"I've seen a few myself. And while I appreciate the camaraderie, let's not do that again."

"Very well," Emmet replied. "Then we will take it easy, eat hardily, share a cup, and get you on your feet."

"A very different approach than most Quartermasters I know."

"Firstly, we are not on a ship, nor do I think you would be drunk while on duty. Secondly, Olav deals with those matters and his method involves a lot of cold water."

"Then I thank you for the coffee." He tipped his cup to Emmet. "Your handling of drunks shows clear experience."

"Oh…I had lots of practice, long before I went to sea," he said, his normally nervous demeanor starting to return.

"Yes." Roger grimaced, rubbing his brow. "I think I remember you saying your father is a sot."

"Sot of sots!" Emmet declared through a mouthful of food.

Roger chuckled and took another sip.

A rap sounded at the door.

The two looked at each other, unsure who would be knocking.

Emmet felt panic rise and shook his head nervously, thinking of every terrible scenario possible, including some he was sure Roger would not fathom.

The knock came again.

Roger carefully stood and gave his attire a quick glance. Nothing but a shirt and trousers. In an attempt at decorum, he pulled his waistcoat on, then answered the door.

Lt. Samuels appeared on the other side with a look of relief. "Superb. You are here."

"Lt. is there a problem?"

Emmet saw Lt. Samuels glance, past his commander, toward him. He returned a nervous hello.

"Your mother sent word to the ship, thinking you were there, and when we informed her that you were not, because we assumed you were at the estate…"

Roger leaned into the door frame and sighed. "She sent you to find me."

Lt. Samuels nodded.

Roger cleared his throat. "I apologize. I was not in a condition to return to the ship or…home."

Lt. Samuels examined him and gave Emmet another glance. "You appear better now."

"Yes…I will send word to my mother before she sends the rest of the Navy to find me."

Lt. Samuels' face wrenched in consternation.

Roger's brow furrowed. "How many men are looking for me?"

He scratched his head. "Only half a dozen. Your mother was very convincing that you were in danger."

"Better question," Emmet squawked. "How'd you find us?"

Lt. Samuels looked directly at Emmet. "A local said there was an officer singing songs with some lanky Scot all night in the local tavern."

Emmet laughed. "Curse of small towns."

Roger leaned an arm against the door frame and ran his hand over his face once more. "Call them back to the ship, please. Hopefully, this does not get back to Russell."

"Nothing so far, I assure you."

Roger straightened his spine, releasing an audible exhale. "Allow me a moment to collect myself. I will be down momentarily."

The Lt gave the disheveled room another glance and then replied, "Yes, Sir. I will send word and wait for you downstairs."

Roger quietly picked up his boots and began to dress.

Emmet put the tray back on the table. "I hope I did not cause any trouble, by not letting you go home last night."

"No," Roger replied. "Likely not." He started to button his waistcoat.

Emmet could clearly see Roger regretting his actions, which meant any deviation from normal expectations was not something others saw. Yet, Emmet knew Roger was not so strict, because only a man of passion and individuality would defy a whole fleet and let them escape.

Emmet knew what happened in the captain's chambers. He was listening. He also knew what he and Old Smith were doing on the Daughter's Fortune long before anyone else. He saw the letter and the fine clothes. The minute Old Smith told him that they were lady's things, he knew the man was lying.

When he discovered that they were incognito, Emmet said nothing, because at the time it did not cause any harm and if Jeaneau had found out...she certainly would not have trusted Roger.

Before this whole Gustave business, Emmet was certain

those two were destined. His mind wandered over how he was going to write Gustave into the story, but knew his task would be easier than any of Jeaneau's future choices. Or Roger's.

Roger put on his hat. "Quartermaster Crumbs, thank you for seeing to my well-being."

"Pleasure?" Emmet replied.

"No, I should make it up to you. If there is anything you need during your stay, please let me know."

Emmet grinned, remembering his writing. "Just your company. Perhaps you can tell me what happened after you jumped off the ship?"

Emmet watched Roger recall the incident and studied the myriad of emotions. The man felt something for the captain. Perfect fuel for a forbidden romance, at least on the page.

Roger and Emmet entered the main hall of the inn and spotted Lt. Samuels, who immediately stood and bowed.

"Lt.," Roger said, "this is the Quartermaster of the Daughter's Fortune, Mr. Crumbs. Emmet, this is Lt. Samuels, my second in command."

"And life," the Lt added with a smirk. "So you are the lanky Scot?"

"Yes?" Emmet squawked.

"Did you send w—" Roger began but was cut off when the front door burst open, and Adah rushed to her son.

Beholden to no decorum, she wrapped her arms around Roger's waist and hugged him.

"Mam, I'm okay," he whispered.

She then smacked him in the arm. "I am not!"

"Mam, I'm sorry," he implored. Captain in the Navy and reduced to a child in his mother's presence. "Perhaps we can discuss this more privately?"

"Yes, on the way home."

Roger shook his head. "I am not going back to the estate."

"You most certainly are!"

"No."

His mother stared up at him with intense fury, making him feel very small.

He sighed. "I will walk you home."

TWENTY-FIVE

Breaking of the Ice Floes

Olav and his wife slowly packed his bag. They rolled his clothes in tight tubes and pressed each one snuggly in the satchel.

"Please be careful." Elise sighed, worry in her voice.

"I will. The Captain is savvy," Olav assured her with a soft squeeze.

"I know she is, but the French are using the deposing of King James to push at our borders. We may be a free state, but…" She was unable to control the shiver that ran down her spine.

Olav kissed the top of her head in a soothing manner, and let his head rest there for a moment. "Nations fight. It is what they do.

She shifted to stare at him and cupped his face. "And men die."

"I'm not a soldier, Elise."

Her eyes darted with worry. "But you are sailing into dangerous waters."

He drew her hands into his. They were tiny and delicate in his massive palms, a pool of light surrounded by night. He gently kissed each finger. "I promise, as I always do, to return home."

"Alive," she asserted.

"Alive, my Elsikede," he promised, tenderly kissing her lips.

"Must you go?" Gustave implored.

"You made a promise," Jeaneau replied in a playfully sassy tone.

He pulled her away from packing. "But hasn't it been nice? Just us. Here. No torrential seas, no turmoil, and no rations."

She smiled and kissed him softly. "The food is tempting."

"Just the food?" he asked, rubbing his hands over her hips.

"Mmmm," she mused. "Yes," she replied and bopped a kiss on his nose, then went back to packing.

He sunk into the bed. "But what will I do while you are gone?"

"Work?" she snarked.

He looked away, despondent. "I suppose."

"Oh, don't pout. I know for a fact that you have a line of ships waiting to be tended to. Plus, Father will be here soon enough to help go over construction plans for the new warehouse."

"He is not the Elricksen I wish to spend my time with," he said, impishly tugging at her skirts.

"I've been here for months!" she protested.

He let out a long sigh. "Is it too much to want to be with my wife?"

"I will see you in Marseille in April," Jeaneau replied, still trying to maintain a relaxed tone.

"Must I wait so long?" he whined, clutching his hand to his chest and looking forlorn.

She rolled her eyes, now getting frustrated. "We had an agreement."

He sat up. "Yes, I just thought…"

She exhaled very slowly and stepped away. "Don't make me feel guilty about this."

"I'm sorry," he resentfully replied.

She closed her eyes. She was not going to be goaded into another fight. His moods were exhausting. "I need to see to the ship." She began to walk away.

He chased after her and shut the door before she could exit. "Jeaneau…"

She stepped back from him. "I don't want to fight."

"Neither do I," he begged. "I just want you to know that you don't have to leave."

She sighed, but remained resolved. "I know I don't have to, but I want to."

"Why?" he pleaded, stroking her arms delicately.

"Because this is what I love doing and you said you wouldn't stop me," she replied, hurt in her eyes.

"That was before we knew there would be a war," he gently retorted and kissed her fingers. "I'm only thinking of your safety."

She scoffed. "There is always a war brewing and there will be protected routes."

"French or English?" he queried.

She grinned proudly. "Both, actually."

He pulled her into an embrace and gazed at her. "I will worry."

Touching his face, she replied, "I know." then smirked. "The curse of the sailor's wife."

"Oh, so I am the wife now?" He scoffed.

"Yes," she replied with mirth.

"Can a wife do this?" he picked her up and kissed her passionately.

She broke the kiss. "I've had women pick me up and kiss me. You may need to do better than that," she teased.

"Big woman!" he declared.

"I like them big and strong," she replied and nipped at his lip.

"Oh indeed? I think there are a few things I can do they can't." He carried her to the bed.

"Care to show me?" She pulled him in for another kiss the fight averted.

He pinned her down, as he kissed and coaxed pleasure from her.

Jeaneau was lost in a whirl of sensations all designed to distract her. Her sighs became rhythmic and she wanted more.

He stopped and pulled away.

She sat up and looked at him in shock.

He leaned back, his breath heavy, and sneered playfully.

"Why…" she replied, reaching out for him. "Why did you stop?"

He dodged her grasp. "Will you miss me?"

She sighed, hooking her leg around his and pulling. "Yes!"

"Good," he replied, standing up. "Then I will leave you wanting, so you come back as quickly as possible."

She hit the mattress in frustration and disbelief. "What!"

He straightened his clothes, and stared at her with indifference.

"Are you serious?" she uttered. "You have never…" She shook her head, recalling his absolute dedication to her pleasure. "You always…"

"Oh, I know," he replied, softly stroking his throat and reveling in her want.

"You will now!" She huffed and stomped her foot.

"Will I?" The words slithered out of his mouth with malicious torment.

"You will or I will find someone who will," she threatened, refusing to relent. He would not get the upper hand.

He stepped back and leaned over her. She felt his hot breath roll over her neck and down her bodice. He went in for a kiss and retreated when she reached out. "And what will you do for me?"

"What do you want?" she asked, already unbuttoning his trousers.

He stopped her hand and pressed it against the post. "Oh no…not that, not yet…" His other hand gently slid up her leg. "I want your fidelity."

"My fidelity." She gasped, shocked by the request.

"Yes, no man…" He nipped her ear. "No woman…"

She shuddered, feeling his teeth scrape along her neck. Her thoughts became muddled and her breath quickened.

Gustave gripped her braids and pulled back her head. His gaze seared her with lust. "But me."

The desire he invoked was strange and incomparable. It was like skirting between a storm and rocky shoals. Exhilarating, exciting, and wonderfully frightening. She knew he was trying to control her, but the reward was carnal bliss.

His lips hovered inches from hers, but he held her head so she could not close the gap. His breath roll into her mouth. "You are my wife. Say it."

All sense was gone. "I am your wife," she softly moaned.

"Again," he demanded, pinning her other arm when she tried to touch him.

"I am your wife!" she shouted, wrapping her legs around him, throwing him into her.

He bit down on her neck and sucked hard.

Completely at his mercy, she cried out, "I am your wife. Your wife. Your wife." High on the pleasure and pain, she could feel the mark forming and didn't care.

Gustave lifted up from her neck and grinned at her, victorious.

Her wrists pushed against his grasp. "Now do your duty as my husband."

His tongue ran over his teeth and he smiled. "Of course, My Dearest."

Gustave performed his duties and Jeaneau was lost to delight again, unable to tell up from down, and she knew that was exactly where he wanted her.

"Jean-Pierre!" Elrick declared.

"Captain!" Jean-Pierre replied and embraced him.

Elrick pulled away and held him at arm's length. "You are looking well."

"Thank you. I've been well fed this winter."

Elrick squeezed his arm. "I heard a sailor once say, 'If I were rich. I would eat nothing but fat.'"

"I can see that." Jean-Pierre grinned, eyeing Elrick's belly.

Elrick laughed. "Ah, the price of prosperity and old age. So, how is my daughter?"

"Ready to sail," he replied and started them towards the estate.

Elrick released a puff of air in surprise. "A blushing bride so quick to leave her groom?"

Jean-Pierre pushed his glasses back up his nose and retorted, "We both know that the sea is Jeaneau's Mistress, and doubt any will come before her."

Elrick nodded in agreement. "More than once I was sure she would grow a tail and swim away. She still have that bizarre bath?"

"Oh yes, she insists the cold sea is good for her hair and skin," Jean-Pierre replied.

"Can't argue with proof." He laughed.

"I suppose not."

"And how is the new groom?"

"Completely and utterly enraptured with Jeaneau. I truly saw very little of them," Jean-Pierre provided, working not to make eye contact.

"Well then, that bodes well?" Elrick asked, his tone holding an air of concern.

"Yes…" Jean-Pierre replied, then changed the subject. "Are you going to ask about your wife?"

"Is she still here?"

"No, already back in France planning the final stages."

Elrick exhaled in relief. "Then I will leave her to it. If she ever tried, she could run my business better than I or Oliver."

"Oliver?" Jean-Pierre inquired.

"Yes!" Elrick declared and looked behind him.

Jean-Pierre followed Elrick's gaze, seeing a man walking five paces behind them. He was slender, pale, and had hair so light it was almost translucent. His eyes however were intensely dark blue, and off putting.

"Oliver, this is Jean-Pierre. First mate to my daughter. Oliver will be overseeing the build of the new warehouse and running it."

"Pleasure," Jean-Pierre said and put out his hand.

Oliver took it and responded, "And returned. Did you stay at Mr. Oostwal's home over the winter?"

"No, no," Jean-Pierre impressed, then pointed towards the town, "nice little inn, down there. Good way to stay close, but not intrude."

"Would the Innkeeper be inclined to let me take over the rooms?" Oliver inquired.

"I don't see why not. I can escort you there later." Jean-Pierre replied with an extra twinkle in his eye.

Oliver nodded and softly smiled. "Obliged."

Jean-Pierre smiled back.

"Now boys," Elrick interjected, breaking up the interlude, "I would like to see my daughter before she leaps into the sea."

They entered the main house and waited for servants to inform the couple of their arrival. Elrick saw the pair descend the stairs and wasn't sure how to feel about their appearance. She did her best, but her skirts were wrinkled and her hair clearly mussed. He hoped to write it off as nuptial bliss. While unexpected, it eased his worries that she didn't marry simply for strategy.

He knew Avice was pressuring her to marry. He held out hope that Jeaneau would find someone that could match her in wit and be a balance to her temperament. He did not expect that to be Gustave.

Elrick worked with Gustave for years, visiting this port so often it felt like a second home. His inquiries toward his daughter were stacked among the multitude of others, but it still came as a shock when Avice informed him that she had secured a match. More so when Jeaneau agreed.

Gustave was a good union on paper, but Jeaneau was not an easy spirit to tame, nor did he think a man could or should. He was pleased to hear Gustave permitted her to continue sailing and hoped he would be good on his word.

Jeaneau's face lit up when she saw him. Hiking up her skirts high to keep from tripping, she rushed down the stairs, and hugged her father's neck.

Elrick happily embraced his daughter and picked her up so her feet dangled like they did when she was younger. He laughed and then jibed, "You look like you've already been at sea."

She touched her hair and blushed. "Oh…I…No, but I am ready."

He laughed, happy to still see the sparkle in her eyes. "You are always ready to sail."

She smiled and tugged at his coat. "Is that so bad?"

"For you, my dear, no." He chortled and kissed her forehead.

"Can I petition to disagree?" inserted Gustave, as he finished descending the stairs in a dignified manner.

"I fear all part and parcel to this package. You marry a selkie, then you must know she will return to the sea."

"Unless I hide her fur coat," Gustave retorted.

Elrick's hackles rose, eyeing his new son-in-law closely, then exchanged a glance with Jean-Pierre who returned his suspicion.

"Dinner!" Jeaneau interjected. "I'm starving."

Elrick watched his daughter devour her food and recollected visions of Avice desperately trying to impress manners on the child. She did succeed, but when in relaxed company, Jeaneau reverted to eating without restraint.

Gustave leaned over to his father-in-law. "I've noticed she eats as hearty as a man."

Elrick chuckled. "Because she works and is built like one. I'd trust her to hold my lifeline."

"As would I," Jean-Pierre added. He leaned over to Oliver. "I've seen her deadlift cargo with ease that should take two men to carry."

"Perhaps she is eating for two," Gustave suggested.

"Dear Lord, I hope not," Jeaneau blurted and took another bite.

"My Dearest, do you not wish for children?" Gustave asked.

"And what exactly would I do with a child?" she remarked.

"Why, raise it," he replied.

She eyed her husband. "Where would I raise it?"

"Here?" he said, unsure there was any other answer.

She lightly smacked the table. "And that is why I will not have any."

"What?" he said in mild shock.

Jeaneau sawed into her meat and took another bite. "If I am to only raise my child on land, then I will not have any."

"You can't possibly think of raising our children at sea," Gustave stated in disbelief.

Jeaneau shrugged and drank her wine. "Why not? I was."

Gustave looked to Elrick for help.

"She is right," Elrick replied. "She was raised at sea. Perhaps not the safest choice, but..." He smiled at his daughter. "I got to see my children grow up. Most sailors do not."

"Because it is absolutely dangerous," Gustave spat. "I will not have my children put in that kind of peril."

"Which is why I will not have any," Jeaneau answered and continued to chew.

"You can't stop God's will and I deserve an heir," Gustave said, raising his voice.

Jeaneau rolled her eyes. "Men and heirs."

The rest of the table stopped eating, fearful of what to do next.

Elrick's eyes darted between the two. This was his concern. A man had a better chance of controlling a tempest than his daughter. "Perhaps in time," Elrick suggested.

"No," Jeaneau firmly stated. "My choice."

The whole table could see Gustave turn red with anger, but before he could lose his temper Jeaneau stood, tossed her napkin on the table, and said, "I will be on my ship."

Elrick stood and faced his host. "Gustave, I do apologize for my daughter's behavior, but she can be rather...forthright in her convictions."

Gustave glared at Elrick, still fuming. "Yet, she is no longer your daughter, but my wife, and she will learn."

TWENTY-SIX

Too much Salt Water will Kill You

*J*eaneau stretched in her cabin bed and sighed. Her feet and hands thumped against the raised edges, designed to keep her from rolling out in rough waters, but she didn't care. It was familiar and she was alone. She leaned over, pulling a book from the cubby below, the one she leant Roger. Andromauqe by Racine, a horrifying tale of passion gone wrong. No wonder Roger was so curious about her views on love. She touched the cover softly, then unbound the ribbon ties.

A whiff of the hothouse flowers from Gustave floated up her nose. She glanced over at them and grimaced.

The note replayed in her head.

I'm sorry, My Dearest.

Please forgive me.

I spoke with the vigor of a man wishing to build a life with you.

I did not mean to upset you.

Please sail safe and I await the day you are secure in my harbor again.

Your husband, Gustave.

She huffed, barely married and already an issue. Their last

conversation buzzed in her head and all the flowers in the world would not convince her to stay home and make babies.

It was not supposed to be like this. She picked him because of his nonchalant and liberal attitude. Apparently, that only applied to him and what he wanted. The minute they were married an anchor was lashed to her leg and weighed her down. Demands of fidelity, obedience, and children. Plus even though he promised, he clearly did not want her sailing.

She looked down at the book again and threw it against the wall. Torrid passion and betrayal was not the thing to read today. Sighing, she instead chose the first volume of Don Quixote. A little fantasy perhaps?

Before she could begin, there was a knock at the door. She bid them enter and saw Lance.

Jeaneau sat up and smiled. "Welcome back."

He bowed. "It is good to be back. I am here to check you before we sail."

"Of course." She put the book down and sat up.

Lance began his examination and Jeaneau immediately saw his concern.

"Oh, don't mind those," she said, about the marks on her neck, "Gustave said, 'just something to remember him by'."

"And your arms?" Lance inquired. "If I didn't know better, I would say you were working the ropes."

Jeaneau pulled down her sleeves. "Price of wanton pleasure?"

Lance continued his examination and Jeaneau became aware of all the marks and bruises. She paid little attention to them in the heat of the moment, so much pleasure in a little pain. Yet, the way Lance reacted to them made her see them differently. No longer tokens of passion, but sigils of ownership.

He finished and stepped back. "Overall you are healthy, but the bruising." He hesitated. "Is he hitting you?"

"No!" Jeaneau declared. "Truthfully we are just rather...vigorous."

He did not seem convinced.

"Possibly a little rougher than I am used to, but merely an over exuberance of desire."

"If that is what you enjoy, then I will say no more. However"–he pulled out a salve and a pouch of tea–"use this for the bruising and drink this twice a day. It will help bolster the blood and you will bruise less."

Jeaneau took the items. "Thank you."

Lance bowed and left.

Standing, Jeaneau walked over to the mirror and pulled back her collar. The marks were large and splotchy, with deep purple centers and long streaks of brilliant green. Old bruises lingered under new ones. She became aware of the pain associated with them and started to feel nauseous. Pressing her hands to her face, she exhaled, "What have I done?"

TWENTY-SEVEN

Playing Dice with The Fates

$\mathcal{E}$mmet stood on the pier, watching the Daughter's
Fortune slip into the harbor and dock. He anxiously
paced, waiting for the landing platform to connect.

"Mr. Crumbs!" Jeaneau bellowed from the ship. "You pick
the strangest places to rest. Next thing you know, we will be
picking you up in Scotland."

"Never there!" he squawked. "I assure you."

He motioned for them to come to shore.

Jeaneau and Jean-Pierre came down the ramp.

"Besides, weren't we supposed to meet on the other side of
this damnable country?" Jeaneau complained.

"As I said in my letter, circumstances changed, and I would
be delayed. Easier for you to come to me."

"Why?" Jeaneau queried.

Emmet did his best to hide his enthusiasm and secret
machinations. "A wedding!"

"Pardon?" Jean-Pierre asked, clearly suspicious.

"A wedding," he repeated and started walking.

"Who do we know that is getting married"–she looked
around–"in Wales?"

"Uhhhh, you don't," Emmet stammered.

Jeaneau looked at him like he was mad.

"But I do and, well, you kind of do," he said, forcing a toothy grin.

Jean-Pierre smacked Emmet's shoulder lightly. "Make sense."

"No time," Emmet squawked. "You are late. I will tell you on the way."

Jeaneau and Jean-Pierre looked at each other in bewilderment.

"Good. Good," said Emmet and continued down the street.

His companions followed, working to keep his pace.

"Mr. Crumbs, report," Jeaneau demanded.

"Okay…well…" he said excitedly. "A friend's mother is getting married. Huge thing. She's marrying a local lord and they have been in love for over 25 years!"

"What friend, Emmet?" Jean-Pierre asked.

He stopped and wrung his hands. "Well…I would say he is a friend. Certainly, to me now, once a man sleeps in your bed, they are surely your friend."

"Mr. Crumbs!" Jeaneau and Jean-Pierre bellowed in unison.

Emmet squawked loudly and covered his head. "It's Young Smith!"

"Come again?" they both replied in a serious tone.

He peeked through his hands. "It's Young Smith. You know, Captain Roger Edevane. His mother is getting married."

"To whom, never mind that does not matter. Besides, except for being a minor acquaintance, why would he care if we are there?"

"He doesn't…know?" Emmet replied nervously.

Jeaneau came to a dead stop. "Emmet this is making no sense."

"When does Emmet make sense?" Jean-Pierre retorted.

"I…uh…hmmph! Look! She is a very lovely lady and he's quite tolerable in that stodgy old man sort of way and when she marries!" Emmet rattled his hands in emphasis. "Young Smith will no longer be a bastard!"

"But why are we coming?" Jeaneau huffed.

He turned and resumed his quick pace. "Because I was invited and you are late, so now you are coming."

He walked them all the way up to a gated estate. The entrance was decorated in flowers and ribbons, beckoning them to the festivities ahead. They continued up the path to a grand house with its own chapel. People milled about the outside, and just as they approached, the crowd burst into cheer. Not to them of course, but the nuptial couple exiting the chapel doors.

Emmet joined their cheers and pointed out Adah and Edwin. Behind them, ducking his head as he exited, was Roger.

Emmet quickly turned to see Jeaneau's reaction. She was entranced, and with good reason. Dressed in a fine sea green coat with silver white trim and a smile from ear to ear, Roger was a feast for the eyes.

Jeaneau jerked slightly, and her face changed to surprise. Emmet glanced back to Roger confirming that he saw her, and she saw him. Emmet could barely contain his excitement.

That is until he felt a hand grab the back of his collar and wrench him away.

"What are you conspiring, Crumbs?" Jean-Pierre hissed.

Emmet flailed trying to regain his balance. "Whatever do you mean?"

"Don't be coy with me. You are up to something."

Emmet jerked himself free and straightened his coat. "Nothing!"

"Are you docking him?"

Emmet's jaw dropped. "No!"

"Is he docking you?"

"Jean-Pierre,"–Emmet smacked his chest, shocked at the insinuation–" what would give you that idea?"

Jean-Pierre stated in a slow and clipped manner, "You said he slept in your bed."

"He was drunk and passed out. He slept in my bed, not we!" Emmet was utterly insulted.

Jean-Pierre narrowed his eyes. "Is this about the bet?"

"No." Emmet's voice wobbled.

"Bet is off. She is married."

"I know," he squeaked.

"Then what are you doing?"

Emmet sneered. "Gustave?"

Jean-Pierre groaned. "I know, but not our decision."

"When did marriage matter to her anyhow?" Emmet declared.

Jean-Pierre sighed. "It is not our place."

"Well…" Emmet said, trying to come up with a solution, "maybe he can just be a very…good…friend."

Jean-Pierre grimaced and looked over Emmet's shoulder.

Emmet turned and found Jeaneau and Roger speaking politely. "See, good friends."

"I swear, Emmet, if this breaks her heart…"

"I know, I know." He waved his hands in mock surrender. "I'll get thrown overboard."

"No," Jean-Pierre hissed, "I will keel haul you."

Emmet yelped in fright.

Jeaneau stood enamored, seeing Roger step out of the chapel, and then panic set in. She was married and had made a promise. Pushing down her feelings, she slipped on a smile, refusing to punish Roger with cruelty in order to protect herself.

He carefully approached her, stopping briefly to shake hands and exchange polite words.

Jean-Pierre stood behind her with Emmet discussing something, but she couldn't hear them over the cacophony of celebrants.

He finally made it to her and smiled. "Captain Elricksen, I did not expect to see you."

"Nor I you. It appears you came across my quartermaster."

He nodded. "Yes, he is staying in town."

"And you with him?"

Roger shifted his weight. "Excuse me?"

"He mentioned you were in his bed."

Roger lowered his head. "Yes, well. I was awfully drunk."

"I told you before. I do not judge. But do you think it is wise?"

"Wise?" he asked, slightly confused.

She walked them away from the crowd. Her thoughts left her own matters and were of him and repercussions. "I am fine with it. You know the rules of my ship, but you do have a buggery act here. And Emmet is terrible at keeping secrets."

Roger's eyes bulged. "No!" he blurted, then lowered his voice. "No, you misunderstand. I merely had too much to drink and passed out."

"Oh!" she softly declared. "Then I am so sorry if I implied… I will make sure it does not get misconstrued. Being an officer, I am sure."

"It is punishable by death," he grimly answered.

"You will have to forgive Mr. Crumbs. He says things in the strangest manner."

Roger grinned. "Yes, I know. Speaking of which…would it even be considered illegal…based on their true nature?"

Jeaneau thought for a moment. "Well…technically…I

guess not. It could still cause Emmet serious issues, but…as far as anyone is concerned, he is who he says he is."

"Yes, I would not want to cause him any endangerment. As for his wording…I've noticed Mr. Crumbs unknowingly dances that line more often than he should."

She giggled. "I suppose he does."

He smiled, which led into a moment of awkwardness. "I…" Roger said, "I should return to the festivities."

"Yes! Mr. Crumbs said your mother is getting married?"

"Did. Just now."

She looked over. "Obviously."

"I had invited Mr. Crumbs. There is plenty to eat if you care to stay?"

"I'm sure your parents would not want unwanted guests on their special day."

"Unwanted? You are never unwanted," Roger affirmed.

Jeaneau felt her face flush and noticed Roger get nervous.

"I mean to say," he began, working to cover his unbridled words, "I have spoken of you, and I am sure they would like to meet a lady captain." He stepped to her side and politely motioned her towards the reception.

They entered the great hall of the manor and a million smells slammed into her. Food, sweat, flowers, and ale mingled with the musky heat of so many in one place. Being the first party she was attending for the season, the smells were a reminder why she always sought fresh air.

Roger lightly touched her elbow, bracing her. "Are you okay?"

"Yes…just the scent. A little stronger than I remember."

He nodded. "I don't like it much either. Give me a fresh walk outside or on the upper deck any day."

Nodding in agreement, she swallowed back rising bile. Reaching into the slit in her skirt, she fetched a small tin and popped it open. She rubbed it under her nose, and the smells were weakened by peppermint. Roger watched curiously, so she offered.

He took a small amount and sniffed it. "Rose and Peppermint?"

She grinned, already feeling relief.

He placed it under his nose and massaged the rest into his hands. "Thank you."

"Lance. Genius with herbs. He's cook, surgeon, and apothecary in one."

Roger jutted his head in a direction, spotting Emmet with Jean-Pierre.

Jeaneau watched Emmet clumsily knock over a tray and snickered softly.

"Your crew is most assuredly motley," Roger remarked.

She looked at him. "I will take that as a compliment."

He grinned back. "It was. I have only known a military ship, and while it has its own color and charm, it demands discipline and conformity. I didn't know a ship could be otherwise."

"Life at sea is challenging enough, why make it a miserable one?"

"Indeed."

They were spotted by the others, who quickly moved through the crowd towards them. Emmet glowed with excitement. His mouth full of food, he said, "Young Smith, I really love your mother's cooking."

He chuckled. "I am aware."

A third man was with her men. He remained quiet, waiting for Emmet to introduce him. He did not. She looked at Jean-Pierre who gave a small shrug, indicating he did not know.

"My apologies, Captain Elricksen," Roger intervened. "This is Lt. Samuels, my First Mate."

"Aw, I liked how you introduced him to me," Emmet said,

then looked at Lt. Samuels. "Corny, you said something funny."

Lt. Samuels was slightly embarrassed by Emmet's lack of propriety, but softly answered, "He said I was his second in command on the ship, and I said…also in life."

Emmet smacked his arm. "That! Funny."

Jeaneau laughed, allowing all the men to relax.

The energy of the room quickly shifted, as bodies moved aside and cleared the floor for dancing. Immediately, couples began to pair off and line up. The local Dance Master took to the center and asked for requests. The crowd erupted with suggestions.

Jeaneau realized that she was not required to work the room. No man here, save her friends, knew who she was, and therefore had no compunction to court her, or ask her to dance. While she felt a relief, she also felt a sadness that she wouldn't be dancing. Did Gustave even dance? Certainly, he did. The bigger question was, what to do now that she was not obligated to mingle. Her eyes darted for an exit.

Roger leaned into her ear. "Are you well?"

"I…I'm not quite sure," she replied, pursing her lips in confusion.

"Is the smell still bothering you?"

"No…" Her brow furrowed.

"Do you need something to drink?" he offered.

She turned to look at him, astonished by his calmness. "It's just strange."

"What is?"

She motioned to the room. "This. I'm just here."

His feet shuffled and hands fretted behind his back. "Am I making you uncomfortable?"

"No, not you, specifically." She lifted her hands in surrender. "I…don't need to be a coquette."

He shook his head, asking forgiveness. "Jeaneau, I never meant…"

She blinked at his informality.

He corrected himself. "Captain Elricksen, my apologies."

"No, I threw you off a ship. Formalities are not necessary."

He chuckled and grinned.

Jeaneau was happy to see her words disarm him.

"Excluding that fact, it is probably best to remain formal, Captain Elricksen, or is it now Oostwal?"

"For business it is still Elricksen," she stressed. Then she asked, "Will your name change?"

He paused. "I...that is a good question...with the same issue."

She chortled. "Ah, you feel the patriarchal noose as well. Putting aside what we should call each other, what I meant was, I have no reason to be here. No contracts, no obligations, and I am certainly not dressed for a wedding."

"I've said before that I like your blue coat."

"But my hair," she said, touching her woven down braids, secured to her head to fight sea winds and still hidden under her scarf.

"I like the scarf too. Reminds me of the women in Morocco."

She touched the fabric lightly, moved by the compliment. "An Egyptian actually taught me."

He beamed. "It is lovely. And"–he motioned to the floor– "there is no dress requirement for this event."

She took a moment to gaze around the room and could clearly see all stations of class dancing and enjoying themselves. Lost in the beauty of the dancers and music, her hips softly swayed with the rhythm.

"Would you care to dance?" Roger blurted.

Her head turned to him, surprised, not only by the request, but her own excitement. "I...I'm married."

"Married people don't dance?"

"Not that I am aware of."

He again gently motioned out to the dance floor, where his own parents were smiling and swaying. "Not only are they married…they're old," he remarked.

She could not stop the grin he invoked but hesitated, recalling the last time they touched. Her skin flushed remembering his thumb running over her mount of Venus.

"Do the man a favor, Captain," Lt. Samuels interjected. "The fellow dances quite well, though rarely does."

"Same for the Captain," Emmet added, "Lovely dancer! Oof!" He yelped, getting jabbed in the side by Jean-Pierre.

Roger put out his hand. His fingers twitched lightly.

She noted they were both wearing gloves. Perfectly acceptable. Nothing untoward with a simple dance. She put out her hand and he guided her to the floor as a minuet began.

Their eyes locked and as they fell into step, Jeaneau was lost. The touch of his hand, the energy between them, each twist and change of position reminded her of the rhythm in shifting of the sails. Why was she doing this? Why was he doing this? Nothing in his demeanor hinted at a man who would woo a married woman. And still the way he looked at her, the way they danced, like lovers meeting.

Then she saw it, his intention. What he was saying. This would be their one moment. Right here, right now, to carry with him when they part. Something that could have been, but never was. He wasn't stealing it from her, but sharing it with her one last time.

She saw him close his eyes briefly, sealing in the memory as he spun her around, then gaze at her again when their hands clasped. She began to tremble, unable to hold back welling tears. He gently steadied her with the slightest movement and nod, no force, just assurance.

She swallowed and completed the dance. When he bowed, she felt the curtains drop on their act and did the only logical thing possible. She fled.

*L*t. Samuels watched as the Lady Captain curtsied and run away from his friend.

Roger stepped back over to Lt. Samuels and stood at polite attention.

"I didn't take you as someone that would go after a married woman," Lt. Samuels commented.

"I won't," he curtly replied.

"Then…that is it. One dance."

"Worth it," Roger replied without hesitation.

*W*hen Jean-Pierre and Emmet noticed the captain had disappeared, they made a polite exit and returned to the ship. There, they found Jeaneau busy at work preparing to sail on the next tide.

Jean-Pierre knew it would be best to say nothing and fell into line.

Emmet went to retrieve his belongings and returned with a bag and satchel in hand.

Jean-Pierre noticed Emmet pull a letter from his bag and walk towards the captain's quarters.

He grabbed Emmet by the wrist. "What now?!" he hissed and grabbed the letter.

"Nothing! Nothing!" Emmet squeaked. "It's official business!"

Jean-Pierre looked at the letter and saw the royal seal. "What is it?"

"I have no idea!" Emmet said.

Jean-Pierre knew he was lying. Emmet could remove a seal off any missive with the skill of a master thief, but in this case, since it did look official and was not from Roger, he would allow it. He tore the letter from Emmet, gave him another glare, and went to Jeaneau's quarters.

As he opened the door, he could feel the tension in the air. He wavered a moment, then stepped in. "Captain, I have a letter for you."

She looked up. Her eyes darted, curious and worried.

"It has a royal seal."

Oddly, this appeared to ease her worry and pique her curiosity. She took the letter, broke the wax, and read it. Her eyes raced across the message and looked at the additional papers attached.

He watched her shudder and slump into a chair.

"Bad news?" he asked.

She scoffed and handed him the letter.

It was an official writ wavering them from port tax and exclusion from being pressed for supplies, even in time of war. Plus, no ship will be rewarded a bounty for their capture or sinking. The Daughter's Fortune was now untouchable in English waters.

"This…this is amazing," he stammered. "Why are you upset?"

"Young Smith…it's all his doing."

"I don't understand. This is what you were going to ask for."

"Yes, but in the moment, I forgot and he…he promised to negotiate for us. Look" –she pointed– "see here about supplies. The day they came on and we dealt with them trying to confiscate our cargo. He remembered and petitioned for this to not happen again. On my behalf."

She slumped forward and covered her face. "I've made a terrible mistake. I pivoted in haste to avoid one storm and threw myself into the rocks. When"–her voice cracked as the tears came– "there was a perfectly good island right there."

Jean-Pierre squatted in front of her and took her hands. "Jeaneau…"

She sobbed.

"Jeaneau, you and I both know that would not have worked. He's English and you are now technically French."

"I know…but the way he looks at me. The way he makes me feel…" She sniffed. "He sees me, Jean. Me. And the respect!" She choked. "Never, not once, did he see me as a woman playing in a man's role. Never. And don't lie. I even had to win you over."

Jean-Pierre nodded, stroked her head softly and held her hand until she stopped crying.

She sniffed hard one last time, lifted her head, and straightened her cuffs. "No, you are right. Our course is set." Jeaneau stood, forcing Jean-Pierre to quickly lift himself out of his squat and step back.

"Monsieur LeGalt, have us ready to sail at tide," she commanded, voice stern and clear.

"Aye, Aye, Captain," he said and started to turn but stopped to lean in and kiss her cheek.

She grabbed his hand and gently squeezed.

He walked to the door, but paused one last time. "And Captain, don't worry, we will figure out how to sail safely off the rocks. I promise."

She swallowed and grinned. "Thank you."

About the Author

Cheryl L-G Trent is a dyslexic neurodivergent Historian from Texas/Oklahoma. Despite limitations, her passion for writing never waned. Being the daughter of a sailor and accountant, and the mother of a cook and artist her knowledge is diverse. She is also a member and raising members of the LGTBQIA+ community. Cheryl loves to write about stories skirting famous events and specializes in Ancient, Medieval, Native American and Clothing History. Additionally, she loves to tell stories of the interlopers and outcasts. The parts of history not written in books but did exist. Her goal is to share fun, adventurous stories that express the struggles of women, outsiders, and the invisible.

Website:

https://www.clgtrent.com/

Cheryl's Linktree:
https://linktr.ee/clgtrent

instagram.com/clgbutterfly

amazon.com/stores/Cheryl-L-G-Trent/author/B0BV1D1N1X

www.ingramcontent.com/pod-product-compliance
Lightning Source LLC
Chambersburg PA
CBHW020024310726

48970CB00007B/2192